After slamming into the barbed wire at sixty miles per hour, the car spun around as the front tires shredded into useless masses of smoke and rubber. Sliding across the bridge backward on the car's front rims, Lex pulled hard on the wheel and managed to spin back around. What was left of the front bumper now faced forward again—and headed right for the young man standing on the bridge.

KA-BASHHH!

The car plowed directly into Clark, crushing him against the guard rail, which instantly gave way. Car, railing, and Clark Kent sailed through the air for what seemed to Clark like endless minutes, then one by one each hit the water and disappeared beneath the surface, sinking toward the murky bottom below.

Clark's eyes closed and everything went black.

SMALLVILLE™

ARRIVAL

MICHAEL TEITELBAUM
Based on the teleplay

**Superman created by
Jerry Siegel and Joe Shuster**

www.atombooks.co.uk

An *Atom* Book

First published in Great Britain by Atom 2002

A CIP catalogue record for this book
is available from the British Library.

ISBN 1 904233 22 8

Typeset by Palimpsest Book Production Limited,
Polmont, Stirlingshire
Printed and bound by
Bookmarque Ltd, Croydon, Surrey

Atom
An imprint of
Time Warner Books UK
Brettenham House
Lancaster Place
London WC2E 7EN

To the comic book writers and artists who brought the Man of Steel to life in my youthful imagination; to George Reeves, who taught me how to fly; to Alfred Gough and Miles Millar for their wonderful story; and to Sheleigah, as always, for watching the shows with me and reading the drafts.

1989

A cluster of meteors, all that remained of a once great planet, streaked through the silent void of space like a pack of hungry predators seeking prey. Billions of brilliant stars sprayed across the rich black tapestry, silent witnesses to the unspeakable force of the approaching onslaught.

Upon reaching the edge of the Milky Way galaxy, the meteor shower picked up speed, its sickly green glow flashing past stars and planets. Entering the edge of a tiny solar system in a remote arm of the spiraling galaxy, the cluster of jagged rocks—some as big as small moons, others no bigger than baseballs—rushed past the system's outer planets.

Ignoring the tiny frozen planet farthest from the system's sun and the huge ringed planet on the outer rim of the solar system, the meteor shower rushed toward the sun at the center of the system with increasing urgency.

Nestled in the midst of this raging maelstrom, a tiny metallic spaceship kept pace with the meteors, protected by them from the ravages of space. Inside the ship, escorted by the meteors like a dignitary with an honor guard, the last surviving member of a doomed race rushed toward the third planet out from the system's sun.

Skimming the lifeless, crater-filled surface of the planet's single moon, the meteors and the ship streaked toward an inevitable encounter with the planet, which its inhabitants called Earth.

CHAPTER 1

The town of Smallville, Kansas, was proud of its status as the Creamed Corn Capital of the World, as the sign at the edge of town boasted. Out-of-towners passing by might chuckle at the accolade, but to its 25,001 residents, the small farming town, which rested in the center of America—in every sense of the word—was something to be proud of.

Only a three-hour train ride from Metropolis, one of the nation's largest cities, Smallville might as well have been on another planet, frozen in time. Life still centered around Main Street, as it had for two hundred years. Generation after generation used the same bank, gas station, and library. The water tower that rose high above Main Street had been casting its shadow down the center of the street in the late afternoon for as long as anyone could remember.

The children of the children of those who worked at the tiny post office fifty years ago were themselves selling stamps and sorting packages. Kids still hung out at Slam's, the local diner, or caught a movie at the Swan Theater, a deco palace that had seen better days and now offered second-run double features.

Vast golden cornfields stretched in every direction, shimmering in the honey-colored sunlight. Farmers bounced along dirt roads on tractors, the day's lengthy list of chores before them. A typical day in a typical American town where very little ever happened, and things rarely changed.

Until now.

WHUP-WHUP-WHUP-WHUP!

The thunderous roar of a helicopter engine shattered the tranquil morning. Its rotors whipped furiously, creating a swirling wind, sending the tall cornstalks bending in all directions. On the side of the speeding yellow chopper, the logo *LUTHORCORP* glinted black in the morning light.

Inside the helicopter, the pilot leaned back toward the two passengers. A man in his mid-fifties with long graying hair and a crisply tailored suit flipped impatiently through the day's copy of the *Daily Planet* newspaper. Beside him sat a nine-year-old boy with soft pale skin, piercing blue eyes, and a mop of unruly red hair.

"We're almost there, Mr. Luthor," the pilot said, turning back to the view out the chopper's front windshield.

Lionel Luthor, owner of LuthorCorp, was a self-made businessman with a considerable fortune. He had built his company up from a small chemical distribution firm into the largest pesticide manufacturer in America. But even that was not enough for this cold, ambitious man.

With his sights always set firmly on growth and increased profit, Luthor was about to close a deal that would expand his massive reach into this pastoral area.

Lionel glanced away from his paper to see his son gripping the sides of his seat, eyes tightly shut.

"This has got to stop, Lex," Lionel said firmly. "Open your eyes, now!"

Lex Luthor squeezed his eyes even tighter and shook his head, his curly locks bouncing back and forth. "I can't," he cried. "I'm afraid of flying."

"Luthors aren't afraid of anything," Lionel shot back through clenched teeth, his meager attempt at patience.

"We don't have that luxury. We're leaders, and we've got to lead by fearless example."

Lex's eyes remained shut, his head shaking faster.

"You have a destiny, Lex," Lionel continued. "But you're not going to get anywhere with your eyes closed. You are a Luthor. You must face the world boldly, with eyes wide open, ready to overcome all challenges."

He leaned close to his son's ear. "This helicopter is not landing until you've looked out that window," he whispered calmly, though the underlying anger was not lost on the boy. Lionel sighed, shook his head, then resumed reading the paper.

Slowly, Lex released his white-knuckled grip on the seat. His father was always telling him in subtle and not-so-subtle ways how disappointed he was in his only son, the heir to his vast empire. Why should this day be any different? Other kids could be scared, but not Lex. Other kids could ask their fathers to give them a break, show a little understanding, realize that they were only human, only nine years old. Other kids weren't Luthors.

Opening his eyes and turning toward the window, Lex looked down at the sea of corn rushing past him with blinding swiftness. The dizziness struck first, his whole world spinning and shaking, then came the tightness deep in his chest. *Here it comes!* he thought, fumbling for his inside jacket pocket.

He tried to draw a breath, but his throat closed with the effort. Gasping and wheezing, Lex gulped desperately, trying to suck in air, any air, to no avail. His trembling fingers finally grasped the inhaler in his pocket. Pulling it out and turning away from the window, he pumped—one, two, three—sprays of the lifesaving medicine deep into his lungs.

The tightness passed. Lex breathed deeply again, filling his oxygen-starved lungs with cool air.

Lionel leaned back in his seat, disgusted at the boy's weakness.

"Is your boy okay, Mr. Luthor?" the pilot asked, turning once more to the passenger cabin.

"He'll be fine," Lionel replied, smiling, avoiding any eye contact with his son. Then he crisply snapped open his newspaper and flipped the page.

The helicopter began its descent toward the Ross Creamed Corn factory, whose better days had clearly been left behind. Peeling paint and broken windows suggested there were once more prosperous times. A nearly empty parking lot revealed jobs lost and families moved away. Two brothers, Dale and Bill Ross, stood outside the factory, looking up at the gleaming chopper, shielding their eyes from the sun.

Here, in the creamed corn capital of the world, the Ross brothers had always been the kings of creamed corn. But these days times were tough, and the factory that had made the product for decades was losing money fast.

"Here comes the future," Dale said sadly, gesturing toward the helicopter.

"He's not going to change anything," Bill assured his brother. "He gave us his word, remember?"

Dale continued to stare at the copter, which gently landed in the factory's parking lot. He grimaced and shook his head. "Lionel Luther is the pesticide king of Metropolis," he blurted out. "What the hell does he want with a creamed corn factory?"

"Don't worry, Dale," Bill said, clasping his brother's shoulder. "We really need this money. And I'm sure Mr. Luthor is a man of his word."

ARRIVAL

In a flower shop on Main Street, a woman busily added a small handful of baby's breath to a bouquet she was completing. Her attention was distracted by the tinkling of the tiny bell on the front door to the shop, indicating the arrival of customers.

A handsome couple in their mid-thirties strolled in. The dirt on their jeans and boots and the rugged, weathered skin of their faces made it evident to anyone in this town that they were farmers.

"Afternoon, Nell," the man said, nodding to the women who had just finished creating the bouquet, his thick blond hair sprinkled with gray falling onto his forehead.

"Jonathan!" Nell exclaimed, a broad toothy smile expanding across her face. She spotted the woman who had walked in behind Jonathan. "Martha," she added, her expression dimming slightly, the disappointment unmistakable in her voice. "This is a surprise. What brings the reclusive Kents to town?"

"Tulips," Martha replied, flashing a big grin of her own, her pretty freckled face surrounded by long red hair. "Red ones, if you have them."

"Well," began Nell, putting down the bouquet and opening the glass door to the refrigerated case that held her cut flowers. "If you're looking to add some color around that farmhouse, what about a tiger orchid?" Nell had never gotten over her high school infatuation with Jonathan. Her pretty but weary face reflected hard, lonely years and many regrets.

"Thanks," Jonathan replied. "But Martha had her heart set on tulips."

Nell shrugged. "Makes sense," she said, pulling a handful of red tulips from the case. "They are a very uncomplicated flower."

Ignoring the barb, Martha turned her attention to a dark-haired young girl sitting at a table near the back of the store. Dressed in a princess costume, complete with a billowing white dress and a jeweled tiara, the pretty three-year-old waved a glittering magic wand.

Recognizing the girl, Martha joined her, kneeling down so they were face to face. "That's a beautiful dress, Lana," Martha said enthusiastically. "Are you a princess?"

"I'm a fairy princess," Lana corrected her. "Do you want to make a wish?"

"I'd love to make a wish," Martha replied, closing her eyes.

Lana waved her wand over Martha's head three

times, then gently touched her on the forehead with the star on its tip.

"Lana, be careful," Nell called from the front of the shop. "You'll poke somebody's eye out."

"Thank you, fairy princess," Martha said, bowing. Then she pointed to some toys on the table. "What else do you have there?"

Jonathan watched silently as Martha played with Lana. The look of longing in his wife's eyes was not lost on him. "Where are her parents?" he asked Nell.

"Homecoming game," she explained. "Along with everyone else. I'm being the good aunt, watching her. I'm surprised you're not there, Jonathan, reliving your glory days."

"I like to think that my best days are ahead of me," he said, looking at Martha, who smiled appreciatively.

"Martha," Nell called out. "Has Jonathan ever mentioned that we were homecoming king and queen in our senior year at Smallville High?"

"No, he hasn't," Martha replied. "But thankfully, you slip it into every conversation, just so we all remember."

As Jonathan took the flowers from Nell, the Kents

turned to leave. "Good-bye, Princess Lana," Martha said, bowing once again.

Outside on Main Street, Jonathan and Martha climbed into the cab of their pickup truck. Martha stared out her window, deep in thought.

"I know what you wished for in there," Jonathan said, putting his arm around her. Their inability to have children had never interfered with the depth and closeness of their relationship. Theirs was a strong marriage, molded from mutual respect and the hard work and long hours of running a farm. Jonathan loved her with all his heart, and Martha knew it.

His high school romance with Nell had been fun. He was the star of the football team, she was the homecoming queen, full of spirit and mischief and a sense of adventure. But his love for Martha was as solid as the bedrock beneath his cornfields.

Still, he knew how much she longed for a child, and he ached for her.

"I looked at Lana's little face, and I . . ." Martha let her words trail off. "It's all I ever wanted."

Jonathan leaned close and kissed her warmly on the mouth.

HONK! HONK! HONK!

The tender moment was interrupted by the blaring of car horns. A crowded convertible sped past, filled with screaming high school students waving cheerleading pom-poms and banners that read "Smallville High" and "Go Crows."

"Looks like Smallville won again," Jonathan said, putting the truck into gear and driving off toward their farm, as the victory celebration continued on Main Street.

♋ ♋ ♋ ♋

Miles above the earth's surface, the meteor shower neared the end of its long journey. Piercing the planet's upper atmosphere, flames surrounded each rock, trailing behind in a brilliant red tail of fire. The surface of the meteors glowed green, the color growing in intensity with each passing second.

Still traveling in the center of the storm, the spacecraft sliced through the atmosphere, its front heat shield protecting the sole passenger on board. Searing flames surrounded the craft, glowing reddish orange, extending into a long, streaking tail.

This massive assemblage of fiery destruction was now only moments away from slamming into the earth.

✆ ✆ ✆ ✆

At the Ross Creamed Corn factory, Lionel Luthor was about to sign the papers that would transfer ownership of the factory and its surrounding cornfields from the Ross family to LuthorCorp. He leaned against an old pickup truck, flanked by Bill and Dale Ross, using its hood as a desk.

From the corner of his eye, Lionel spotted Lex tossing a small stone at a crow perched on top of a cornstalk. "Lex!" he bellowed, shouting his disapproval, wondering when his boy would grow up and start acting like a man. Then he turned back to the papers. "Now, gentlemen, where do I sign?"

After reviewing the contract for a final time, Lionel Luthor signed the deal.

Lex, meanwhile, dropped the remaining stones from his hand and turned away, completely bored, as usual, watching his father nail down a deal. He knew he was supposed to be interested in the business of LuthorCorp, but he was tired of his "destiny," and just wanted to be a regular kid.

Shoving his hands into his pockets, Lex wandered

into the cornfield. Hidden by the tall stalks that towered over him, he trudged along a furrow between two rows of stalks, his head bent low.

A weak voice cried out from nearby. "Help me!" it gasped feebly.

Looking around, Lex saw no one. Stepping forward, his feet crunched the dry corn husks scattered on the ground. *Must have been the wind,* he thought.

Again the faint voice cried out. "Help me! Please!"

Looking up, Lex spotted a scarecrow. *Is the scarecrow talking to me?* he wondered. *How can the scarecrow talk? This is really creepy. I'm getting out of here!*

He took off, dashing back through the field, fear gripping his mind. Then his chest tightened in the terrible, familiar signal that another asthma attack was about to strike. Lex began to wheeze and gasp for breath. Reaching into his pocket, he grabbed his inhaler. As he lifted it to his mouth, he tripped over a broken cornstalk and tumbled to the dirt, the inhaler flying into the tangled mass of corn.

Desperately groping among the dirt and husks, crawling on his hands and knees, Lex searched in vain for the life-giving apparatus, finally bumping into a thick wooden post that had been driven into the ground.

"Hey, kid," the strained voice cried out again. "Help me!"

Looking up, Lex found himself staring into the face of what appeared to be an odd-looking scarecrow. Squinting through the blinding sun, Lex saw that this was not a scarecrow at all, but a teenage boy. The boy was tied to the post by a thick rope, his feet bound together, his arms tied to a crosspiece near the top. Dressed only in his boxer shorts, the boy had a red letter "S" painted on his bare chest in crude, thick brushstrokes.

Panic washed over Lex. But before he could move, a huge orange fireball streaked through the sky, passing directly overhead with a deafening roar.

"Help me, please," the captive boy mumbled one last time.

THOOOMMM!!!

Lex leaped to his feet as the first enormous meteor slammed into the center of the cornfield and sent shockwaves radiating in all directions. Running as hard as he could, Lex ignored the burning in his chest.

Spotting a thick trail of black smoke outlining

the course the incoming projectile had taken, Lex glanced back over his shoulder and saw a huge shock-wave flattening everything in its path. The air around him rippled, charged with vast energy, then a wall of debris moved toward him with incomprehensible speed.

Dirt, smoke, and debris propelled by an unimaginable force struck the post and its prisoner first, snapping the wooden stake like a toothpick, slamming the teenager into the earth, face first, still a captive of his ropes.

Despite the hopelessness of his flight, Lex pressed on. Within seconds, though, the shockwave caught up with the terrified boy and lifted him off his feet, tossing him high into the air amidst a swirl of choking gray dust, buffeting winds, and, finally, only blackness.

A crowd quickly formed on Main Street, drawn from homes and shops by the unearthly sound and violent shaking. The revelers who just seconds earlier had been waving pom-poms and screeching with joy jumped from their cars to watch the long black smoke trail arc across a perfect blue sky.

Clutching Lana tightly in her arms, Nell rushed from

the flower shop. "What on God's earth is going on?" she asked, staring at the thick plume above.

At that moment, Lewis and Laura Lang, Lana's parents, stopped their car on Main Street, across from the flower shop. Stepping out, they spotted their daughter. Lana saw them at the same moment.

"Mommy! Daddy!" she cried with glee, waving with one hand, clutching her magic wand tightly in the other.

With all eyes turned skyward, the entire town looked on in horror as a second cluster of meteors appeared above, streaking toward the center of town. The first meteor crash and the resulting shockwave had been only the first taste of the immeasurable destruction that was about to change Smallville forever.

Nell started toward the Langs, then stopped and stared in disbelief as a flaming chunk of rock from above headed right for Lana's parents. The three-year-old followed the path of the fiery missile with her eyes.

"What's that pretty light in the sky, Aunt Nell?" she asked, seconds before the meteor slammed into her parent's car.

KA-FOOOMM!

The car exploded in a smoky, flaming fireball, vaporizing the Langs instantly. The force of the blast threw

Nell and Lana into a rack of flowers displayed outside the shop. Windows along Main Street shattered, and terrified townspeople fled for their lives.

Climbing to her feet, still holding Lana, Nell peered into the girl's face and saw only terror and confusion. One second this three-year-old was without a care in the world. The next, she watched as her parents were killed by a rock from space. Lana's tears mixed with black soot from the explosion; her horrified screams were unheard amid the commotion.

FOOM! FOOM! FOOM!

Obliterated by a meteor, the water tower high above Main Street showered thousands of gallons of water onto people below. Another meteor demolished the Welcome to Smallville sign, leaving only a smoking stump behind. Still they came, raining flaming destruction from the sky.

One searing chunk tore a hole in Town Hall, entering the landmark building on one side and emerging from the other before finally opening a crater in the sidewalk.

Cars and trucks on Main Street bounced into the air like toys, crashing and shattering in the smoke-filled street. It seemed that the assault would never end.

❧ ❧ ❧ ❧

Lionel Luthor raced into the cornfield he had just purchased, shouting, "Lex! Lex! Where are you?" Pausing, he realized that the entire cornfield, extending for acres in all directions, had been flattened, as if a great scythe has swooped through and hacked each stalk at its base.

Stunned by this sight, Lionel stepped forward and spotted a tuft of red hair on the ground. Kneeling, he picked up the thin, charred copper-colored strands, realizing their full implication. Was this all that remained of his only son?

A pile of cornstalks just ahead shook slightly, and Lionel dashed to it. Stripping away the seared shoots, he saw Lex curled on the ground in a fetal position, trembling uncontrollably, sucking in short, sharp breaths.

Lionel turned away in revulsion. All the hair on Lex's head—those beautiful curly red locks—was gone. At the age of nine, his son was totally bald. Cradling Lex in his arms, Lionel walked slowly from the field, his son still trembling, and headed back to his helicopter, anxious to depart this wretched little town.

ഇ ഇ ഇ ഇ

Jonathan Kent mashed down on the gas pedal of his pickup as the battered old red truck sped along the highway.

Martha spun around in time to see a meteor slam into the blacktop of the road behind them.

"What's happening, Jonathan?" she asked, her eyes widening in fear.

Whirling around for a glimpse of the damage, Jonathan didn't see the spaceship crash into the road right ahead of them until it was too late.

THOOM!

After ramming into the ground only yards from the truck, the glowing-hot spacecraft carved a trench as it slowed to a halt some 300 yards from its point of impact.

Jonathan slammed on the brakes, sending the pickup veering into the thick black smoke pouring from the crater before them. They flipped over and landed in a ditch among the rubble.

Dangling by their seat belts, hair brushing the roof of the upside-down cab, the Kents slowly regained consciousness.

Jonathan's eyes fluttered open, his head throbbing, his vision blurred. As the upside-down world came into focus, he saw what appeared to be a naked child, a boy maybe three years old, walking on the charred, smoldering remains of what had been a cornfield.

Barefoot, Jonathan thought, disregarding for the moment logical thoughts of how and why and what. *He's walking barefoot on burning ground,* was all his mind could register.

"Martha," he called, his voice gruff and dusty.

It was Martha's turn to force open heavy eyelids and fight through the thick haze in her head. She, too, saw the handsome boy with thick brown hair squatting to peer inside the truck.

Before either of the Kents could speak, the boy casually grasped the passenger's door and yanked it off the truck in one smooth, effortless motion. Gently easing herself out of the seat belt, Martha rolled from the cab, then struggled to her feet.

Scampering around to Jonathan's door, the naked tot repeated his casual feat of strength, tearing the door away in one swift move, as if he were unwrapping a birthday present. As Jonathan groped his way from the cab, he saw that Martha already had the boy wrapped in a blanket and cradled in her arms.

"You all right?" he asked.

"Yeah, you?" Martha replied.

"Fine," Jonathan said quickly, realizing that they were both avoiding the obvious. "Kids don't just fall from the sky," he said after a pause.

"Then where did he come from?" Martha asked. Now that they were actually discussing the subject at hand, she was ready.

"I don't know," Jonathan replied, as they carefully walked through the smoking wreckage. "But he must have parents."

Stopping short, the Kents looked down at the small metallic spacecraft, which was half buried in the trench where it had come to rest.

"If he does," Martha said, nodding at the ship, "they're definitely not from Kansas."

"Sweetheart, we can't keep him," Jonathan said, sighing, knowing exactly what his wife was thinking. This was not going to be easy. "What do we tell people? That we found him in a field?"

Smiling at the boy, Martha stared into his clear, blue eyes. He mimicked her expression, grinning broadly. Then she turned to her husband. "We didn't find *him,* Jonathan," she pointed out. "*He* found us."

CHAPTER 2

Jonathan and Martha Kent brought the boy home to their farmhouse. Having decided to adopt and raise him as their son, they vowed to tell no one about the bizarre circumstances of the boy's arrival. If anyone asked, they explained that Martha's sister had passed away and left the child in their care.

Storing the spacecraft in an old storm cellar on the edge of the property, Jonathan made sure the evidence of his new son's origin was well hidden. Later, venturing into one of the seedier sections of Metropolis, he would acquire a fake birth certificate, just to give everything the appearance of normalcy. The only thing as important to the Kents as raising their son was making sure that no one ever learned the truth about his arrival on Earth.

The Kents named the boy Clark, Martha's maiden name, and took great joy in watching him grow. Bit by bit, they discovered that the strength he had displayed in freeing the couple from the overturned truck was just the beginning of his amazing powers.

By the age of four, Clark could easily lift the living room couch with one hand. When he got excited and ran, he circled the 100-acre property in less than five seconds. While playing in the barn at age eight, a large metal milk can toppled right onto his head. Clark emerged without a scratch.

The Kents kept all this a tightly guarded secret, fearing that if the authorities found out their son had dropped in from another planet and possessed unusual abilities, they would take him away to analyze the boy and treat him like a living science experiment or an alien freak. They kept Clark out of any organized sports activities or play groups, fearing not only that his secret would be exposed, but that he might accidentally hurt another child.

When he was old enough to understand, they told Clark that he was adopted. They also told him that he had to keep his special powers a secret. They made no mention of his arrival, his spaceship, or the details of how he had been discovered that day. As a kid, Clark simply accepted what his parents told him, thinking it was pretty cool that he could do all these amazing things, without giving the subject too much thought.

Smallville itself changed dramatically in the years following the meteor shower. It was dubbed "America's Weirdest Town" by a national news magazine, and it seemed that strange, unexplainable things were always taking place in the quiet hamlet that seemed so normal on the surface.

Bizarre occurrences—such as the 150-pound tomato that took first prize at the state fair, the golden retriever that gave birth to a two-headed puppy, and the miraculous recovery of a critically ill woman given no chance to survive by her doctors—became increasingly common in Smallville.

Some were sure that the meteor shower was the cause of these strange events. Others blamed LuthorCorp, which arrived in town that same year, turning the Ross Creamed Corn factory into a high-tech fertilizer plant.

Having been destroyed by a falling meteor, the "Welcome to Smallville" sign was rebuilt, its slogan changed to: "The Meteor Capital of the World." The population grew as well, from 25,001 to 45,001 in the twelve years following the horrific events of that fateful day.

The years zipped by quickly for the Kents, the plodding pace of farm life keeping them always busy. Dealing with Clark's powers was at times difficult, but for the most part it became something the three of them were able to cope with.

When Clark entered puberty, however, his powers increased dramatically, unpredictably, and sometimes uncontrollably. Along with the normal changes that any human teenager experienced during this time, Clark's secret abilities became harder and harder to keep under wraps, and the young man grew more and more frustrated at the limitations his parents placed on his use of these increasing powers.

As with all teenagers, Clark longed to feel normal, to fit in. He was also very curious about his unique abilities, often wondering if there was anyone else in the world who could do the things that he could do.

There was not.

☞ ☞ ☞ ☞

Fifteen-year-old Clark Kent stared at the Web page displayed on his computer's monitor. His clear blue eyes darted back and forth at an incomprehensible pace, as he absorbed article after article about unusual people displaying incredible powers.

There was the six-year-old Korean boy who lifted a car off his father, who was trapped beneath it, the record-breaking teen who had just been declared the fastest human alive, and the African tribesman who survived a blazing fire with barely a scratch.

Always searching for others who might be gifted like he was, Clark had many such stories bookmarked, and still his search went on.

Although he knew he had to catch the school bus, the high school freshman sat at his computer in a T-shirt and sweatpants, the clothes he intended to wear to school that day still hanging in his closet. His room was a mess, with magazines, CDs, and school books scattered around the floor, desk, and bed. He knew he couldn't let his mother see it this way, but that would not be a problem.

"Clark Kent!" Martha called from downstairs. "You are going to be late for the bus!"

"Okay, I'm coming," Clark yelled back, but he didn't move. He was intent on finishing three or four more articles before he got dressed, cleaned his room, grabbed some breakfast, and scooted out to meet the school bus.

Martha Kent bounded up the steps to once again pry her son from his room.

When Clark heard the handle on his door begin to turn, he figured it was time to get moving. Flipping off his computer, he removed his T-shirt and sweats, pulled on his school clothes, including shoes, combed his thick brown hair, then tidied up his room, filing his CDs in alphabetical order, stacking the magazines, loading his backpack with papers, and grabbing an armful of school books—accomplishing all of this before the handle completed its full rotation and the door to his room popped open.

"Welcome to Tuesday, Clark," Martha said, sticking her head into the room. "If you're all dressed and your room is straightened, then what are you doing up here? Come down for breakfast."

"Morning, Mom," Clark replied, smiling. This had become a familiar ritual for mother and son.

Martha held up a dark blue suit on a hanger covered with dry-cleaning plastic. "It's one of your father's," she explained.

Clark look at her, puzzled. "Did someone die?" he asked only half-seriously.

"Homecoming dance this weekend," she reminded him. "Remember?"

"I don't have a date, Mom," he said, looking away. "I figured that would be the big tip-off that I'm not going."

"Did you ask anyone?" Martha wondered.

"No," Clark replied, shrugging.

Sighing, Martha turned to go hang the suit up in Jonathan's closet. "You see, asking someone is kind of the critical step to landing a date, Clark," she said, trying to make it sound supportive rather than sarcastic.

"It's not a big deal, Mom," Clark replied, following his mother out of the room.

"I just wish you'd let people see who you really are," Martha said as they headed down the stairs. Stopping, she turned back to him. "I mean, you know, on the inside. Not—"

"It's okay," Clark said, smiling. "I know what you mean."

Reaching the kitchen, Clark threw open the

refrigerator door, grabbed a bottle of milk, and took a long swig, all in one motion.

Martha was not amused. She snatched the bottle from his hand and placed it on the table, then gave Clark that "Mom" look, which he knew so well.

"What?" Clark said, with just a hint of a whine. "It tastes better out of the bottle."

"Where did you learn your manners?" Martha asked.

"On a farm?" Clark replied, finishing her classic question, then turning away to hide his smile at having the perfect response.

Jonathan Kent stepped through the front door into the kitchen, peeled off his dusty jacket, and grabbed the bottle of milk from the table. He'd been up since dawn doing the chores that were just a matter-of-fact part of life on a farm.

"Good afternoon, sleepyhead," he said to Clark, then he lifted the bottle to his lips and guzzled down three or four deep gulps of milk.

Clark flashed his mother a quick smile—like father, like son—then sat at the table, nervously fingering a small slip of paper.

"Now, don't forget, you two," Martha began, placing plates of bacon and eggs in front of Jonathan and Clark.

"I've got class tonight, so you're on your own. That means, don't order pizza! There's plenty of food in the fridge."

Father and son shared a momentary guilty look over the success of Martha's apparent mind-reading ability. *How did she know we were going to order pizza?* Clark wondered.

That's what being married for twenty years does for you, thought Jonathan, taking a sip of coffee, then noticing Clark anxiously turning the piece of paper in his hand over and over. "What have you got there, son?" he asked.

"Permission slip," Clark replied casually, as if this were something that happened every day. "It's for the football team. A couple of spots opened up. They're holding tryouts this afternoon."

Jonathan took the form from Clark's hand and stared at it long enough for Clark to realize that he was not about to get the reaction he had hoped for.

"Come on, Dad," Clark moaned. "You played football when you were in school." It was a good try, but it landed on deaf ears.

"That was different, son," Jonathan replied without hesitation.

"Why?" Clark shot back, knowing the answer all too well.

"You know why, Clark," Jonathan said, placing the permission slip onto the table.

Taking a deep breath, Clark looked his father in the eyes. "What if I run at half speed and never hit anybody?" he asked. The solution seemed perfectly logical to him.

"A lot of things can happen in the heat of a game, Clark," Jonathan explained, the voice of wisdom and experience.

"Look, most new guys don't even get to play," Clark pointed out, grasping at what felt like the thinnest of straws. "I'll probably ride the bench for most of the season."

They locked eyes again. Jonathan wasn't budging.

Clark loved his father but was often frustrated by his stubbornness. "Dad," he began softly, "I can be careful."

"I know you can," Jonathan assured him. "But what if there's an accident?"

Clark looked down at his breakfast, defeated. His father, it seemed, had an answer for everything. He scooped up a forkful of eggs and shoveled it into his mouth.

"Clark, I know it's hard for you." Jonathan finally said, genuine compassion in his voice. "But you've just got to hang in there like you promised."

"I'm sick of hanging in there," Clark said, getting up from the table, pulling on his light tan jacket, sliding one strap of his backpack onto his shoulder, and grabbing the stack of books he had placed near the door. "All I want to do is go through high school without being a total loser." Then he turned and pushed through the door, hurrying out to catch the bus.

Martha slid into a chair next to her husband. "He deserves to know the truth," she said, hurting deeply for her son.

"He's our son. We adopted him," Jonathan said, finishing the last bits of his breakfast. This was a discussion the couple had had many times, but its urgency grew with each passing year. "That's the only truth he needs to know, Martha."

"Today it was football," Martha replied. "Tomorrow it's going to be something else. He's not a kid anymore, and his questions are only going to get harder. Plus, he's changing."

"He's always been changing," Jonathan pointed out.

"Every year he gets a little bit stronger and a little bit faster."

"It's different now," Martha argued. "Last week I caught him lifting a tractor. Having these powers isn't fun for him like it was a few years ago. It makes him different, and that can be a terrible strain in high school."

Jonathan put down his fork and looked at his wife. He couldn't deny the wisdom in Martha's words, and he felt badly for his son's position as a "loser," but he knew that the great secret the family shared had to remain hidden from the rest of the world.

"You and I have always been together on this, Martha," he said slowly.

Martha clasped his hand tightly. "There are three members of this family," she said. "And now that he's a young man, Clark's feelings have to be taken into account."

"What if he tells somebody?" Jonathan asked. "I don't want anyone showing up, flashing a badge, and taking him away from us."

Martha got up from the table. "If we don't tell him the truth soon, nobody will have to take him away," she said. "He'll leave all by himself."

Outside, Clark shuffled along the driveway, his backpack slung over one shoulder, his head down. *How could they possibly know what I'm going through?* Clark thought as he slowly made his way toward the road. *Dad was a football star at Smallville High, and Mom grew up in Metropolis, far from small town cliques and labels. Neither of them had to contend with life as a loser, not to mention being a freak.*

Jolted out of his thoughts by the sound of the school bus pulling away from the road at the end of his driveway, Clark shouted, "Wait!" Racing to the end of the driveway, he saw the bus's tail lights disappear around the bend. "Aw, nuts!" he muttered, feeling even more sorry for himself. What else could go wrong today?

Suddenly, a broad smile spread across Clark's face. He turned and dashed into a nearby cornfield, moving at astonishing speed, a wispy blur trailing a cloud of dirt behind him.

༓ ༓ ༓ ༓

On the school bus, two of Clark's best friends settled a bet.

"I can't believe you bet against your best friend, Pete," said a pretty blond-haired girl dressed in a long vintage coat trimmed with a fake fur collar, as she handed a five-dollar bill to the boy in the seat next to her. Her bright blue eyes sparkled with intelligence, her easy smile lighting up her face. She wasn't happy about moving to Smallville from Metropolis, but her father's job brought the family to this quiet burg, and as she had always done, Chloe Sullivan made the best of it.

"It's a statistical fact, Chloe," Pete explained, pocketing the bill. His close-cropped hair circled his soft-featured face, and his black T-shirt peeked out from the top of his gray button-down shirt, which was topped by a flaming red jacket. "If Clark Kent moved any slower, he'd be extinct. I knew he would miss the bus. He always does. Easy money, my friend."

Pete Ross was the youngest of a long line of overachievers. His older brothers had all been athletic stars at Smallville High, and the display case in the school's lobby held the awards and trophies to prove it. Pete felt he could never measure up to them, and so he never tried, choosing instead to shield himself with a quick wit and a contagious smile.

The bus rumbled along the thin strip of blacktop that

paralleled the cornfield that had once belonged to Pete's family, but now was part of LuthorCorp. Both Pete and Chloe had a connection to the field and to the Luthors. Pete's family had once owned the land, and Chloe's father, Gabe Sullivan, was recently transferred to Smallville to serve as plant manager of Lex Luthor's fertilizer factory.

If either of the two friends had bothered to glance out the window at that moment, they would have noticed a strange trembling along a line of tall cornstalks as an unseen force streaked through the rows, passed the slow and steady bus, and raced toward Smallville High.

By the time Chloe peered out her window the rippling force had sped past. All that was visible were endless rows of corn. "I couldn't take living on a farm," Chloe remarked. "It's so, so Amish." Chloe viewed herself as an urban sophisticate, exiled to small-town American while her father ran the fertilizer plant. Her dreams stretched beyond the cluster of farms, fields, and recently constructed planned communities, to the big city and the world of newspaper journalism. For the time being, she settled for her role as editor of Smallville High's newspaper, the *Torch*.

"I'll let you in on a little secret, my friend," Pete began. "That little planned community of prefab plastic Monopoly houses you call home used to be a farm." Pete remembered when the farms began to disappear and give way to the developers and their instant communities. Then there were all the stories his parents told him. The Ross family had been in Smallville since 1870, and felt a strong personal connection to the town and its history.

When Lionel Luthor broke his promise to the Rosses twelve years earlier and turned their creamed corn factory into a fertilizer plant, the family felt powerless and betrayed, and wanted little to do with the Luthors from that point on. The majority of Smallville felt the same way.

"Smallville isn't home," Chloe explained. "It's a forced layover on my way back to Metropolis, and a job at the *Daily Planet*."

Pete shook his head and slumped down into his seat, laughing softly. *Chloe and her dreams of glory,* he thought, realizing that though he teased her about it, this was one of the things that made Chloe so attractive to him.

The speeding blur tore through the backyard of a

house right next to Smallville High, sending the wet sheets hanging on a clothesline billowing furiously in an explosive gust of wind.

The streak slowed gradually, then stopped, leaving Clark Kent standing in front of Smallville High, clutching his school books. A satisfied smile spreading across his face, Clark gazed up at the red-brick-and-white-stone structure, a banner for the homecoming "Fly to Victory" dance flapping in the cool morning breeze.

After turning into the large parking lot, the school bus squealed to a stop and released the boisterous students, who bounded out and headed across the playground. Chloe strode quickly, a few steps in front of Pete, who rushed to catch up.

Pete looked at Chloe, swallowed hard, then took a deep breath. "Anybody ask you to the dance?" he finally said.

"Not yet," Chloe said flatly.

"Well," Pete continued, "if nothing pans out with you-know-who, I thought—"

"Pete," Chloe cut him off. "How about you take a small commercial break from the soap opera in your head. I'm not interested in Clark!"

Pete nodded. "Your vehement denial is duly noted," he said.

Chloe stopped and turned toward Pete, sighing in exasperation, her breath sending locks of blond hair dancing in front of her forehead.

Pete flashed a big bright smile at her. "So, maybe we could go to the dance together," he suggested. "Not as a date-date thing," he added quickly, "but, you know, more like a friend-friend thing." Pete was dying to ask Chloe out on a real date, but his shyness and insecurity, plus his belief that she had a huge crush on Clark, kept his advances in the joking, teasing, and friend-friend mode.

Before Chloe had a chance to respond, Clark came trotting up behind them. "Hi, guys," he said casually.

Pete and Chloe spun around, stunned to see their friend. "Didn't we just see you miss the bus?" she asked, squinting at Clark in astonishment. "Weren't you just . . ." her voice trailed off.

"I took a shortcut," Clark explained, as if that simple statement cleared up the mystery.

"Through what?" Chloe asked, in her best tough-guy, news-reporter voice. "A black hole?"

"You'll have to forgive our intrepid reporter," Pete

chimed in. Having grown up with Clark and been his best friend since elementary school, Pete long ago learned to expect the unexpected when it came to his buddy. "Her weirdness radar is set on defcon-five."

Chloe looked from Clark to Pete, then back to Clark. "Just because everyone chooses to ignore the strange things that happen in this idyllic little hamlet doesn't mean they don't happen," she said forcefully.

"Look, Chloe, we'd love to join you and Scooby in the Mystery Machine for another zany adventure," Pete began, clasping Clark firmly on the shoulder. "But Clark and I have to hand in our permission slips before homeroom."

Clark's body tensed up, his lips pressed tightly together. He hadn't even thought about what he would tell Pete. "Actually, Pete," he began, thinking on the spot, "I'm having second thoughts. I don't think signing up for the team is such a great idea." As close as he and Pete had always been, Clark's powers had to remain a tightly guarded secret, even from his best friend.

Pete stepped right in front of Clark and looked up, shaking his head. *To what do we owe this sudden change of heart,* Pete wondered. *Yesterday he was all gung-ho about joining the team.* "Clark, I'm telling you," he said tersely. "It's the only way to be sure we're safe."

Chloe's jaw dropped in amazement, and her gleaming blue eyes opened wide. "Wait!" she shouted. "You two are trying out for the football team? What is this, some sort of teen suicide pact?"

Grabbing Chloe by the shoulders, Pete guided her to a quiet corner of the playground. He glanced left and right to make sure no one could hear what he was about to say. "No," he whispered nervously. "No suicide pact. We're both trying to avoid becoming this year's scarecrow."

"What are you talking about?" Chloe said softly. "And why are we whispering?" she shouted, her voice growing louder with each word.

Pete waved his hands, signaling to Chloe to lower her voice. "Shhh!" he said, index finger against his lips. Then he continued, speaking quickly in a low, anxious voice. "It's a homecoming tradition," he explained. "Before the game, the football players choose the geekiest freshman, take him out to Riley Field, strip him to his boxers, and paint an 'S' on his chest."

"Then they string him up in the middle of the corn-field like a scarecrow," Clark added.

"Geez," Chloe said, repulsed by this bizarre male ritual. "Sounds like years of therapy waiting to happen."

Pete nodded, looking around again. "That's why we're trying out for the team," he whispered. "We figure they won't choose one of their own." Revealing this dirty little school secret to anyone, much less to the editor of the school newspaper, could have serious consequences, making his high school career a living nightmare. But he trusted Chloe completely.

"Why don't I write an article in the *Torch,* exposing this twisted, back-country ritual?" Chloe suggested. *One more reason to get out of this cow town and back to a real city as soon as possible,* she thought.

"Not a great idea, Erin Brockovich," Pete replied, wondering now about how complete his trust in her should be. "Some of us actually want to get through freshman year in one piece."

Clark glanced over his shoulder toward the entrance to the school building. He spotted a beautiful girl with long, gleaming brown hair, sparkling almond-shaped eyes, full red lips, and a smile as dazzling as sunshine.

Losing all interest in the conversation at hand, Clark looked back at his friends. "I'll see you guys in class," he mumbled, then turned and strode toward the vision in the blue sweater that set his heart pounding.

"'Bye," said Chloe, laughing softly to herself.

Pete pulled out the five-dollar bill he had won earlier and held it up to Chloe's face. "I give him ten seconds," he said.

"Five," she replied, taking the bet.

As Clark walked slowly away, Pete counted. "One, two, three, four, five!"

Now only three feet away from the beautiful girl, Clark stumbled as if he had run into an invisible wall, tumbled into the bushes that lined the outside of the school, and watched his books scatter in all directions.

"Just like clockwork," Chloe said, snatching the bill from Pete's fingers. "It's a statistical fact. Clark Kent can't get within five feet of Lana Lang without turning into a total freak show!"

Embarrassed by this latest bout of unexplained clumsiness in Lana's presence, Clark scrambled to his feet and began picking up his books. He had known Lana for as long as he could remember. From the first moment he showed interest in girls, Lana was the girl he most wanted to be with. By this time, his childhood crush had grown into genuine deep feelings for her, feelings he kept hidden along with his more unconventional secrets.

Lana lived with her aunt Nell, in a house right next to the Kent farm. On the surface, the little fairy princess had blossomed into a gorgeous young woman who was poised, confident, a top student, a popular cheerleader, and already a school leader in just her freshman year.

But gazing into her eyes, Clark sometimes thought he saw hidden pain, doubt, and a deep well of sadness. Watching your parents die instantly, crushed by flaming death from the sky, was not something one got over very easily. He desperately wanted to help her, to get close to her, but whenever she was around, Clark got dizzy, lost his sense of balance, and broke into a chilling sweat.

He reached for the last book on the ground, but a delicate hand grabbed it first. Looking up, Clark gazed into Lana's deep brown eyes. Then he noticed her necklace, a small green stone set in a silver base, attached to a thin silver chain. Clark wiped the sweat that had suddenly formed on his forehead with the back of his hand.

"Nietzsche, huh?" Lana remarked, handing him the philosophy book. "I didn't realize you had a dark side, Clark." To Lana, Clark was the boy next door. A nice guy and reliable friend with whom she had grown up. If she had any deeper feelings for him, she gave Clark no indication.

"Ah, well," Clark replied, trying to clear his parched throat. "Doesn't everybody?"

"Yeah," Lana admitted, handing Clark the book, her hand brushing against his, making him sweat even more. "I guess so. So which are you, man or superman?"

"I, uh, I," Clark stammered, trying to come up with a clever response on the spot. "I haven't figured it out yet."

The two friends stood and smiled at each other. A sweet moment for Clark, despite the feeling of nausea washing over him. The moment was quickly shattered.

"Lana!" called a loud deep voice. "There you are." A tall student with thick blond hair and a fine-featured handsome face came trotting up to Lana. He wore an athlete's letterman jacket with a red-and-gold

Smallville High "S" glaring from the front and a large black crow—the school's mascot—flying above the word "Crows" on the back. He kissed Lana passionately on the lips as Clark looked on uncomfortably, fidgeting with his newly stacked pile of books.

"Hey, Clark," the boy said when the kiss was complete.

"Hey, Whitney," Clark gasped, feeling weaker by the minute. He sat on a low metal railing, leaning forward, trying to maintain his balance.

An all-state quarterback and all-around big man on campus, Whitney Ellsworth was the school's sports hero and Lana's boyfriend. They were the perfect couple, good-looking, popular, and apparently very much in love.

"So, Lana," Whitney began, pulling a floppy disk from his jacket pocket. "I was wondering if you could do me a humongous favor? Could you check over my English report? I didn't finish it until about two A.M., so I'm not sure about the ending."

Smiling, Lana took the disk from Whitney and slipped it into the pocket of her white jeans. "I bet it's great, Whitney," she said, squeezing his muscular arm.

Whitney looked over at Clark, whose head was now

resting on the stack of books cradled in his arms. "Dude," Whitney said. "Are you feeling okay? You look like you're about to hurl."

"I'm fine," Clark said weakly, struggling to keep himself from falling over. "Just fine."

Whitney picked up one last book that Clark and Lana had missed. "You forgot one, Clark," he said, tossing the hardcover volume. Reaching out to catch it, Clark lost his grip on the other books, sending the entire stack tumbling to the ground once again. Slipping off the railing, he landed on his butt on the hard pavement.

"You okay, Clark?" Lana asked, looking down at the pitiful form sprawled on the sidewalk.

"Yeah, great, Lana," Clark mumbled, nodding. "I'm great." Then he watched as Lana and Whitney strolled away, hand in hand.

CHAPTER 3

The first-floor hallway of Smallville High School was a bustling cacophony of movement and noise. Shouting voices and scuffling feet echoed off the tile walls as the sea of students moved toward their classrooms.

This symphony of sound rose to a peak with the ringing of the bell, which signaled that those still on route were now officially late for class. Within moments, the halls emptied, except for a lone figure standing before a tall glass display case filled with trophies, awards, and framed photographs, monuments to glory days gone by and great achievements on the field of play.

The tall, gaunt student, a freshman judging by his youthful appearance, stared into the trophy case with sunken eyes. Scanning the cluster of awards, he noticed one name that appeared on many—Ross, Pete's older brothers.

The smiling faces of most-valuable players and game-winning heroes—popular kids, jocks, those with power, and those who wielded that power unfairly—stared out at the sullen student. But the time had come to cut the golden boys of Smallville High down to size.

Balling his right hand into a fist, the student drew back his arm, staring right at one particular photo of three happy football players holding their helmets, their faces beaming with confidence and camaraderie.

"Classes have begun, young man," said an unexpected voice from behind.

The student remained still, his focus on the photo in the case.

"Please have the courtesy to turn around when I address you," the older man behind him said. "I may only be the assistant principal, but I am still due a certain amount of respect."

Slowly, the student turned around to face the short, balding man who confronted him. His hand remained clenched in a menacing fist. His face remained motionless, a silent mask of determination.

"What's your name?" the assistant principal asked. "I don't believe I've ever seen you in this school before."

In one swift motion, the student whirled back around

and unleashed a powerful punch, his fist smashing through the glass front of the trophy case and shattering it into thousands of splaying shards, leaving a huge hole in the glass. His hand still in the case, the student unclenched his fist and grabbed the photo of the three football players, pulled it from the case, and grasped it with both hands.

"Are you out of your mind?" the assistant principal shouted. "Put that back right now and come with me to my office! You are in a great deal of trouble, young man!" He reached up and grabbed the student by the shoulders.

Crackling in a jagged blue arc, a huge electrical charge shot from the student's shoulder and surged into the assistant principal's body, as if the older man had touched an exposed wire. The charge flung him across the wide lobby, where he slammed into a wall and crumpled into a motionless heap.

Taking no notice of this interruption, the student sneered down at the photo in his hands, his mind flashing back to the day it was taken twelve years earlier, and his entire being filling with rage.

"It's payback time!" he growled.

Still clutching the photo, he turned from the trophy

case, then walked calmly from the school, crunching slivers of glass beneath his shoes.

ᔪ ᔪ ᔪ ᔪ

A silver Porsche with vanity plates that simply read "LEX" sped past acres of ripening corn, the afternoon sun glinting off its highly polished body. Upon reaching the entrance to LuthorCorp fertilizer plant number three in Smallville, the car slowed a bit, then turned, tires squealing, into the plant's parking lot.

Longtime Smallville residents were still not used to the sight of the high-tech processing plant, the former home of the Ross Creamed Corn factory. But Lionel Luthor cared little for the sensibilities of the people whose lives he affected. His goal was profit, and right at the moment, this little agricultural facility was losing money.

Lionel sent his son to Smallville to run the plant and turn it around financially, to see if the young man had matured and developed a head for business. He was, after all, heir to the Luthor fortune and the man who would one day take the reins of the company Lionel had worked so hard to build. Lionel saw the assignment as a challenge. His son, however, viewed it as some kind of punishment for never having lived up to his father's grand expectations.

Twenty-one-year-old Lex Luthor stepped from the gleaming car and looked up at his new place of business. He was back in Smallville for the first time since getting caught in the meteor shower that, twelve years earlier, had robbed him of his hair and of a sizable chunk of his childhood.

Things had not been easy for Lex, growing up bald from the age of nine. He got used to the taunts and the name calling, the just-loud-enough whispers of "freak," and "mutant." But he was a Luthor, as his father never failed to remind him, and developing a thick skin and a skill for self-reliance were as much a part of Lex's upbringing as the prep schools, garden parties, and polo matches.

The handsome, self-assured young man was dressed in gray T-shirt and a black jacket, setting off his smooth bald head. He hated being banished to this ridiculous little farm town, but if there was one thing Lex Luthor knew how to do, it was make the most of a bad situation.

Thanks a lot, Dad, he thought, turning away from

the view of endless corn rows and walking briskly into the building.

Striding into the office of the plant manager, Lex startled the burly man sitting at his desk, feet up, munching on an overstuffed sandwich.

"Hope I'm not interrupting," Lex said, smiling at the large man in his mid-fifties.

The startled man dropped his sandwich onto the desk, whipped his legs around, and stood, clumsily, wiping the mayo from his mouth with a paper napkin. "Mr. Luthor!" he exclaimed. "I wasn't expecting you until tomorrow."

Lex extended his hand and received a firm handshake. "My father is Mr. Luthor," he said, the smile frozen on his face. "Call me Lex."

"Gabe Sullivan," the man said, tossing the remains of his lunch into the garbage. "Let me give you a tour of the plant."

Lex laughed. "With all due respect, Gabe," he said, shrugging. "You make dung, manure, crap, right? What's there to see?"

Gabe was clearly flustered by his new boss's response. He scratched his head and looked uncomfortably around the office as Lex picked up a framed picture from Gabe's desk. Chloe's shining face beamed out from beneath a mop of blond hair.

"Your daughter?" Lex asked.

"Yeah," replied Gabe, happy for something to talk about. "That's Chloe. She goes to Smallville High. Wasn't too thrilled about moving from Metropolis, but, what can you do, a job's a job, right? She wants to go back some day and be a reporter for the *Daily Planet.*"

"Hmm," Lex groaned, returning the picture to its place and looking around the office. "I'm partial to the *Gotham Globe* myself."

An uncomfortable silence hung in the air. Gabe finally spoke. "Look," he began, sighing. "I know the plant's losing money, and that you were sent down here to clean house, but I think—"

Lex lifted his hand. "Relax, Gabe," he said. "I'm not firing anybody. First thing tomorrow, we'll go through the operating budget and see if we can trim costs without losing any jobs."

Gabe's eyes widened in surprise. "But your father said—"

Again Lex cut him off. "I may be my father's son," he explained. "But I'm not his lapdog. He sent me here to run this plant and to make it profitable again. How I do it is my business."

❧ ❧ ❧ ❧

The crowd filling the bleachers roared as Clark Kent broke the huddle and stepped up behind the center. Looking over the defense, Clark positioned his hands, ready for the snap. Along the sidelines, Lana Lang and the other cheerleaders leaped and shouted, waving their pom-poms and chanting cheers of encouragement.

Clark barked out signals: "Down. Set. Nineteen, fifty-three. Hut, hut. Hike!"

The snap from center slammed into his hands and he shuffled back into the pocket. Smallville trailed by four points with twelve seconds remaining in the fourth quarter. Clark knew that he had to complete this pass or the game would be lost.

He peered downfield as his line struggled to hold off the onrushing defensive behemoths. He looked left, then right, but all his receivers were tightly covered. Glancing up at the clock, Clark saw that only six seconds remained.

Standing at his own twenty-yard line, he tucked the

ball under his right arm and took off down the field. Straightening his left arm, he easily knocked defensive players out of the way. A linebacker ran right into his path, but Clark leaped over his helmet and continued, picking up speed.

One by one, Clark knocked opposing players from their feet, then crossed the end zone with the game-winning touchdown. He spiked the ball into the turf, and the pigskin exploded from the force.

With the deafening roar of the crowd filling his ears, his teammates lifted Clark onto their shoulders and carried him down the sideline in triumph. Spotting Lana, Clark leaped from the pack and landed right in front of her. She looked stunning in her skimpy cheerleading outfit.

"I knew you could do it, Clark," she cried, wrapping her arms around him.

Gazing longingly into Clark's eyes, Lana tilted her head back as he leaned down for a victory kiss.

The crowd chanted: "Clark! Clark! Clark!"

"Clark!" shouted Pete Ross for the fourth time. This time Clark snapped out of his wonderful daydream.

Shaking his head, he realized that he was sitting by himself in the bleachers, with the football team practicing on the field below. Across the field, he spotted Lana, rehearsing with the cheerleading squad and stealing looks at quarterback Whitney, who was calling plays and leading his team through the scrimmage.

Looking up, Clark saw Pete in his football uniform and helmet, all of which appeared to be two sizes too big. Tiny Pete seemed lost between the gigantic shoulder pads.

"Clark, how do I look?" Pete asked, finally getting his friend's attention.

"Like a tackling dummy," Clark replied, standing up and shaking his head, partly over Pete's clownlike appearance and partly out of regret for having to give up his heroic fantasy. "Good luck, Pete. Don't get hurt."

Clark flashed his buddy a thumbs-up sign, then bounded down the bleachers and away from the field.

ᔓ ᔓ ᔓ ᔓ

Lex Luthor pounded his Porsche into fifth gear and rammed the accelerator to the floor, pushing the speedometer toward eighty. Tearing down a narrow country road, he sped away from the fertilizer plant as fast as he could move, the pulsating beat of his car stereo blocking out all thoughts of the new life he had just begun in this nowhere town.

On a nearby bridge, Clark Kent leaned on the guardrail, staring down into the churning river below. How would he ever get through freshman year, much less three more years of high school? He couldn't join the team and seemed destined to be king of the geek squad in this tiny town where once you earned that reputation you kept it for as long as you remained in Smallville.

Was there any way to convince his father that he could be careful? Should he let his parents know how painful it was to watch others kids succeed, to watch Lana falling for Whitney, while he could do so much, yet was allowed to do nothing but stand around on the sidelines? This special power stuff had been fun when he was a kid, but now, well, it seemed to be more trouble than it was worth.

Deep in thought, Clark was oblivious of the large truck barreling across the bridge on the opposite side of where he was standing. The truck carried a large load of barbed wire, coiled into long rolls and held by a strap at the very back of the truck's bed.

As it reached the midway point on the bridge, the truck hit a huge pothole, sending it bouncing violently. When the rear wheels truck the hole, one roll of tightly coiled barbed wire popped free, fell from the truck's bed, and tumbled onto the road, where it rolled a few feet and then came to a stop, running across the lane in which Lex Luthor was driving. The rattling thud of the truck hitting the pothole masked the sound of the barbed wire bouncing free, so the driver continued on his way, unaware of the hazard he had just deposited onto the bridge.

Heading in the opposite direction of the truck, on the same side of the road on which Clark stood, Lex's sports car pushed past ninety miles per hour and showed no sign of slowing down. He zoomed past the truck, oblivious to the danger in the road.

The chirping of his cell phone distracted Lex for a moment. Reaching into his inner jacket pocket to answer the call, his eyes left the road for a split second. When he returned his view to the front windshield, he spied the coil of wire laying across the road, directly in his path.

Lex dropped the phone onto the seat next to him

and grabbed the steering wheel with both hands as he mashed down on the brake with all his strength.

SCREEEEE!!

Clark was startled back to the moment by the sound of squealing tires. Turning in time to see Lex's car skidding out of control, he watched helplessly as it careened toward the coil of barbed wire just up the road from where he stood at the guardrail.

BLAM! BLAM!

Slamming into the barbed wire at sixty miles per hour, the car spun around as the front tires shredded into useless masses of smoke and rubber. Sliding across the bridge backward on the car's front rims, Lex pulled hard on the wheel and managed to spin back around. What was left of the front bumper now faced forward again—and headed right for the young man standing on the bridge.

Lex lifted himself from the seat, adding extra leverage to his foot as it pressed on the brake, but all he could do was watch helplessly as his car sped toward the man frozen with fear, his back pressed against the guardrail.

Their eyes met for a brief moment, the moment in which Lex suddenly knew that not only was he going to crash through the guardrail and end up in the river, but that he was taking this innocent bystander with him.

KA-BASHHH!

The car plowed directly into Clark, crushing him against the guardrail, which instantly gave way. Car, railing, and Clark Kent sailed through the air for what seemed like endless minutes to Clark, then one by one, each hit the water, disappearing beneath the surface, sinking toward the murky bottom below.

Clark's eyes closed and everything went black.

CHAPTER 4

Piercing shafts of sunlight sliced through the churning water, playing across the silver body of the wrecked sports car, which finally came to rest with a gentle thud.

Clark opened his eyes underwater. The shock of what had just happened came over him slowly. Looking down, he ran his hands along his chest, discovering he was unhurt. He found no sign of injury, and he felt no pain, yet he was positive that the speeding car had hit him head-on, knocking him through the guardrail and sending him crashing into the river.

THE CAR!!

The thought filled his head, blocking out the million questions that had flooded his mind in the first few seconds after regaining consciousness. *Must get to the car! What if I'm too late?*

Clark dove, his arms pulling back in a powerful breast stroke, legs kicking furiously, his body shooting downward like a torpedo.

In the driver's seat of the submerged sports car, now nestled among the reedy river bottom, Lex hung, bobbing from his seat belt, unconscious, his cell phone floating past him. The windshield was gone, along with a small section of the roof. The front end crumpled in an accordionlike mass of twisted steel.

Upon reaching the wreck, Clark spied the small hole in the roof. Grabbing the edge, he peeled back the remainder of the roof, tearing it off as if he were opening a can of tuna. Tossing the twisted metal aside, Clark tore open the seat belt, then grabbed Lex with one hand and pulled him from the wreck.

Using his free hand like a paddle, Clark shot to the surface with one powerful stroke. Upon bursting free of the watery prison, Clark quickly swam to shore, careful to keep Lex's head above the surface, though he was uncertain whether or not the man he had just rescued was still alive.

Gently placing Lex onto the ground, face up, Clark knelt over the blue-lipped, motionless form. Lex's face was cut and bleeding, but that was not the primary concern at the moment. Placing his ear to Lex's chest, Clark could not detect a heartbeat. Pinching Lex's nose with one hand, Clark pulled open his mouth with the other and blew in.

Nothing.

Scrambling to the side, Clark placed his left hand on Lex's chest, then put his right hand over his left. "Come on," he shouted, pressing down hard, pumping the chest again and again. "Don't die on me!"

Again, no movement.

Thrusting down hard, over and over, panic setting in, Clark pumped Lex's chest.

Finally, Lex stirred, then spit out a short stream of water and coughed violently.

Clark stopped pumping, his own heart pounding in his chest. Lex gasped, sucked in deep breaths, and then looked up into Clark's eyes, the same eyes he had seen seconds before the crash.

"I could have sworn I hit you," Lex wheezed, then fell into another coughing fit.

"Well, if you did," Clark began, "I'd be . . ." He paused, then looked over his shoulder at the missing section of guardrail, realizing that he really had been hit by the speeding car. "I'd be dead," he completed the thought.

Clark slumped down on the ground next to Lex, the

color draining from his face. He stared at his hands, trembling, as the realization of a new power, possibly his greatest power, struck him with a force equal to that of the speeding sports car. He was not hurt, no broken bones, not even a scratch.

Sure, growing up he had been conked on the head by a metal milk can and fallen down enough times without scraping his knees to realize he could take a good deal more punishment than most people, but to be rammed by a car speeding at sixty miles an hour, smash through a metal guardrail, and plunge into a river, then emerge without the slightest bruise . . . Who was he? *What* was he?

"Kid, are you okay?" Lex asked, pulling himself into a sitting position.

Clark nodded. "Yeah," he replied. "I'm fine."

An ambulance soon arrived, followed shortly thereafter by a towing crane, as a crowd of onlookers gathered on the bridge. The EMS workers bandaged Lex's cuts and offered Clark a warm blanket. He was still in shock, more from the realization that he hadn't gotten hurt than from what should have been a fatal crash—for both of them.

Jonathan Kent's pickup truck screeched to a halt on

the bridge. Leaping from the front seat, he shimmied down the rough gravel bank and ran to the spot where Clark sat. Clark climbed quickly to his feet and hugged his father, genuinely glad to see him, happy for something that felt normal in the midst of this new craziness.

"Are you okay, son?" Jonathan asked, embracing Clark tightly.

"I'm all right, Dad," Clark replied, as his dad stepped back and looked around.

Jonathan spotted a police officer filling out a report. "Who was the maniac driving that car?" he asked the officer.

"That would be me," came the reply from behind Jonathan, before the cop could respond.

They turned to see Lex walking toward them, his right hand extended. "Lex Luthor," he said.

Jonathan looked at Lex, contempt flashing in his eyes. Ignoring the offered handshake, he turned away. "Jonathan Kent," he said coolly, taking off his jacket and wrapping it around Clark's shoulders. "This is my son."

He had never met Lex Luthor, but Jonathan knew all about his father, who had bought up land in Smallville and made grand promises to local farmers, all of which he reneged on, with disastrous results for long-time residents of the tiny town. Jonathan had nothing but disdain for anyone named Luthor.

Lowering his hand, Lex turned to Clark. "Thanks for saving my life," he said. What else could he say?

"I'm sure you would have done the same for me," Clark replied, flashing a tight-lipped smile. It was obvious that his father disliked the Luthors, though he wasn't really sure why.

Lex turned back to Jonathan. "You've got quite an extraordinary boy there, Mr. Kent," he said, as Jonathan and Clark started up the steep bank. "If there's any way I can repay you?"

Jonathan stopped his ascent and stepped back down. Moving close to Lex he replied simply and directly, "Drive slower."

Lex watched as the two men climbed up the bank. A noise from behind startled him, and he whirled around to see the huge towing crane pull his crumpled car from the river. Watching the car dangle like a big fish on the end of a hook, with sheets of water draining from its interior, Lex noticed the roof, torn open like the top of a tuna can.

Could that really have happened? Could the roof

have been peeled back from the impact of hitting the guardrail? Lex was sure he had hit young Kent—he stared right at him as the car crashed. But that was impossible. If Kent had been hit, he would have died instantly. Somehow he survived, and because of that fact, Lex was alive as well, and forever in his debt.

It was a debt that Lex Luthor would not soon forget.

☙ ☙ ☙ ☙

In the kitchen of the Kent farm that night, Jonathan sorted through a stack of bills, while Martha read a book on new organic farming techniques. Clark had been quiet at dinner that evening, shrugging off questions about the accident and staying out of the normal family conversation. After the meal, he went straight to his room, saying he was understandably tired from the day's ordeal.

Martha peered over the top of her book. "Did he tell you what happened on the ride home?" she asked, figuring that if there was something to tell, Jonathan would have already volunteered the information. Still, no harm in asking.

"He didn't say a word the whole way back," Jonathan reported, shuffling papers on the table.

Martha leaned back and shook her head. "Now he's keeping secrets from us," she said anxiously. "He's never done that before. What are we going to do? I don't want to see him grow distant and pull away from us."

Jonathan tossed the bills down onto the table with a bit more force than he had intended. "Unfortunately, our son didn't come with an instruction book," he said, the frustration clear in his tone. "Have you seen the damn feed bill?" he added, shoving papers aside on his desk.

Walking over to the refrigerator, Martha snatched the bill out from under a magnet. "We have to tell him, Jonathan," she said, handing the bill to her husband, who stared back at her silently. "He's searching for answers, and he's looking for them everywhere except in his own home, from the two people who love him the most. We have to tell him."

Upstairs in his bedroom, Clark downloaded and printed out another in a series of online articles about amazing survival stories. But reading about the Indian boy who fell ten stories and lived, the Chinese girl who was trapped underwater for fifteen minutes and survived, or the Canadian man who spent two weeks on a frozen mountain without food, water, or shelter and lived to tell the tale did nothing to answer the burning questions in Clark's mind.

He yanked his T-shirt over his head and looked in the mirror, once again, searching his chest and shoulders for a sign, any sign that he had been hit by a speeding car. Not a scratch was visible.

Clark pulled his shirt back on and quietly slipped downstairs and out the back door. Crossing the property to the barn, he glanced up at the bright, full October moon. Once inside, he climbed to the barn's hayloft, his private sanctuary, his fortress of solitude, as his father liked to call it.

Peering through a telescope, he focused on the moon, scanning the craters, lost in the unearthly landscape. Pivoting the telescope, Clark took in the sweeping moonlit fields, until his view focused on the freshly painted farmhouse on the property next to the Kent's.

Staying with this view, Clark looked on as the front door to the house opened and Lana Lang strolled out into the cool night air and settled onto a swing on the front porch, her legs folded beneath her.

Clark's heart pounded as he pulled his eye from the lens. He smiled for the first time that day, realizing how much just seeing Lana lifted his spirits. He brought his eye back down to the eyepiece and saw the perfect moment shattered as a second figure moved into view.

ᘓ ᘓ ᘓ ᘓ

On the porch, Whitney stepped up behind Lana and threw his arms around her. Her face brightened as she rested her head against his chest. He kissed her cheek, then moved his head around to meet her lips.

"Whitney," Lana sighed, clearly enjoying this. "My aunt will be back any minute." She squeezed his hand affectionately.

"Come on," Whitney whined, brushing her hair away and kissing her neck. "We're living life on the edge. A little danger never hurt anyone."

"If Aunt Nell finds us out here your life won't be worth living," Lana replied.

"Where is she, anyway?" Whitney asked, letting go of Lana and stepping around to the front of the glider. "Bridge club?"

"Lex Luthor's, actually," Lana explained, as Whitney sat beside her.

"I didn't know your aunt was in with the Luthors," Whitney said, genuinely surprised and more than a little impressed. The Luthor name carried a lot of weight in Smallville, though many wished that this wasn't the case.

"She's sold them a ton of land over the years," Lana explained.

Whitney's face lit up. "The Luthors own the Metropolis Sharks," he said excitedly. "Maybe she could put in a good word for me."

Lana smiled. "If you really want someone to put in a good word with the Luthors, you should ask Clark," she said mysteriously.

This was the last thing Whitney expected to hear. "Clark?" he asked, wondering if he had heard her correctly. "Kent?"

"He saved Lex's life today," she explained, the pride in her voice unmistakable. Clark had been her friend since elementary school, and she always thought of him as a sweet guy and a good person. She never would have guessed that the shy boy next door had a heroic side to his low-profile personality.

"You're kidding," Whitney replied, astounded by this revelation.

"Sometimes people can surprise you," Lana said, trying to picture Clark risking his life to save another. "I think it's kind of cool."

"Coach said a scout from Kansas State is coming to the game on Saturday," Whitney blurted out, quickly changing the subject to his favorite one—himself.

"That's great!" Lana exclaimed, genuinely happy for Whitney. She knew how much succeeding as a football player meant to him, and she was always there to support his efforts.

"I just don't want to be another 'remember him?'" Whitney said, a certain sadness coloring his usually strong voice. "Smallville's already got enough of those guys."

Reaching behind her neck, Lana unfastened the clasp holding her necklace in place. "I want you to wear this to the game on Saturday," she said, dropping the necklace into Whitney's hand.

Staring down at the brilliant green stone floating in the silver setting, the quarterback was practically speechless for one of the few times in his young life.

"I can't take this, Lana," he said softly. "I know how much this means to you."

She looked at him confidently. "You can give it back after you win," she offered.

Whitney couldn't take his eyes off the stone. "Is this really made from a piece of the meteor that killed your parents?" he asked, regretting his boldness the moment the words escaped his lips, suddenly uncomfortable at prying into the darkest episode in Lana's life.

"So much bad luck came out of it," she said calmly, not at all fazed by his directness. "There can only be good luck left."

Whitney slipped the necklace into his pocket. He simply had the most incredible girlfriend in the entire world. Leaning in close, he kissed Lana full on the lips.

∽ ∽ ∽ ∽

Back in the hayloft, Clark stepped away from the telescope, his face tightening, his chin falling to his chest. Sitting on a bale of hay, staring down at the loft's wide floorboards, he wondered what else could possibly go wrong today.

CHAPTER 5

As it was for many others in the town of Smallville, Tony Carozza's high school years were the best of his life. A member of the locally famous undefeated Smallville High football team of 1989, Tony enjoyed the privileges of stardom as a small town hero—the girls, the glory, the pats on the back from shop-keepers, the "way to go's" from old folks and kids alike.

Like many of his teammates, Tony was a star in high school, but not quite good enough to play college ball. He never took his classes too seriously. He never had to. As a result, graduation left Tony in a void—not college material either athletically or academically, and stuck in a town with few opportunities.

Fortunately for Tony, he was always good at fixing cars. After high school, he took a few trade school courses and studied harder than he ever had to learn what he needed to work as an auto mechanic. When a full-time job opened at an auto repair shop in Smallville, he grabbed it. He still worked out at the gym three times a week to keep in shape. Things were going pretty well for Tony now.

He was luckier than some of his high school buddies, who ended up in run-down trailers on the edge of town, scrounging for odd jobs and struggling for grocery money. Tony was happy in his work, he made a decent living, and he had managed to come to grips with his past.

Unfortunately, his past had not quite come to grips with him.

Tony tinkered under the hood of a '93 Buick, heavy metal blasting on the screechy boom box in the corner of Frank's Auto Repair. Evening had come, and Tony was beat, having been at it since seven that morning.

Last car of the day, he thought as he slipped around into the driver's seat and turned the ignition. *Come on, baby. Just start, so I can go home.*

CHUK-CHUK-CHUK-VROOOOOM!

The engine turned over and roared to life. Tony smiled and stepped from the car. Gathering his tools, he slammed the hood, revealing a shadowy figure standing in the entrance to the garage, silhouetted by the bright streetlight outside.

Startled by the sudden appearance of this stranger, Tony jumped back, his heart pounding. "Geez, kid," he shouted, catching his breath. "You scared the crap out of me. Look, we're closed. You gotta come back in the morning."

The stranger remained silent and still.

Wiping the grease from his hands with a dirty rag, Tony stepped toward the tall, thin intruder. As he approached the figure, light fell on the stranger's face and Tony stared at him, a glint of recognition in his squinting eyes.

"Hey, I know you, don't I?" Tony asked the teenage boy before him. "You were that scarecrow kid from eighty-nine. Where the hell you been? And how come you don't look any older?"

Standing perfectly still, the boy's wiry frame appeared slight next to Tony's still-muscular body.

"Hey, freakazoid!" Tony said sharply. "I'm talking to you. Wake up!"

As Tony grabbed the boy's shoulder with the intention of shaking him, searing jolts of electric current shot from the boy's body into Tony's hand, engulfing his entire body with crackling blue energy.

The force of the jolt sent Tony flying backward. He crashed into a rolling tool cart and toppled over its shelves, finally landing on his back on the hard cement floor.

"What the hell is wrong with you?" Tony gasped, pain shooting through his shoulder and back, as he lay sprawled on the cold, dirty cement. "Look, kid, that scarecrow stuff was twelve years ago. It was just a game."

For the first time the boy moved, striding menacingly toward Tony, a malicious smile sprouting on his lean, sunken face.

"What do you want?" Tony shouted, still unable to lift himself from the floor.

Kneeling down beside him, the boy stared into Tony's eyes, his smile widening. "It's just a game," the boy said softly. "And now it's my turn to play."

Reaching down, he grabbed Tony's arm, sending another massive jolt of electric power surging into his body. Easily lifting Tony over his head, the boy held him there with one hand as the energy continued to flow into Tony's body, which now flopped wildly like a rag doll.

When he felt satisfied that some small degree of justice had been done, the stranger tossed Tony against the garage's cinder-block wall. Tony's head snapped backward upon impact and slammed into a hanging picture frame, shattering the glass protecting the photograph within.

As Tony slumped to the floor, comatose, the boy glanced at the smashed picture frame and the photo of three smiling football players, identical to the one he had stolen from the display case at Smallville High.

He turned and strolled silently from the garage.

On the morning after saving Lex Luthor's life, Clark got up late for school and, once again, missed the bus. Despite his heroic deeds of the previous day, everything in Clark's life remained the same—or so he thought.

He tore through the cornfield like a tornado before slowing to a stop at the edge of the school's playground, then casually strolled toward the front steps. Each student he passed greeted him warmly, patting him on the back, offering a high five, or calling out to him, "Nice work, Clark," or "Way to go, hero!"

Clark, startled by the fuss, caught up with Chloe and Pete on the top step. "Am I at the right school?" he asked, shaking his head in disbelief.

"Listen to Mr. Modest," Pete said, punching Clark softly on the arm. "You're a full-fledged, official-type hero!"

"Yeah," Chloe chimed in. "How often do high school students perform death-defying rescues. This is genuine big, big news!"

"You are definitely off the scarecrow hook now," Pete pointed out.

Chloe looked right at Clark. "My dad said everybody at the plant is talking about you," she said.

"Well, my dad said you should have let the little bastard drown," Pete added. "That's a direct quote."

"It happened pretty quick, Pete," Clark explained. "It's not like I had time to check ID. Your dad still hates the Luthors so much, huh? He doesn't even know Lex."

Pete looked down at his feet. He was too young to

remember any of the business dealings between his father, his uncle, and Lionel Luther, but growing up he had heard nothing but venom spewed regarding the prominent family. "The Luthors screwed our family, Clark," he said tersely. "My dad doesn't forgive and forget. It's in my genetic code to dislike them."

"Pete," Clark began, putting a reassuring hand on his best friend's shoulder. "It was a business deal, not a Steinbeck novel. I'm sure the Luthors didn't mean anything personal by it."

"Just wait until they come after your farm, Clark," Pete shot back quickly. "Then let's see how you feel about your new buddy."

"Are you kidding?" Clark blurted out laughing. "My dad would never sell!"

"With the Luthors," Pete replied, looking up into Clark's eyes, "he may not get a choice."

Pete turned and strode into the building as two pretty girls waved and smiled at Clark.

"So, how does it feel to be popular?" Chloe asked, noticing Clark's latest admirers.

"Uh, good," Clark replied, his mind still on the two girls who disappeared into the school. "Pretty good."

The praise, smiles, and back-slapping continued

throughout the school day. When Clark arrived home on the farm that afternoon, a brand-new, top-of-the-line, shiny red pickup truck sat in the driveway, a gleaming blue bow tied onto its hood.

Clark dashed up the driveway, then stopped to look over the truck, then spotted Martha bent over a tractor engine, hands full of tools, face covered in grease.

"Hey, Mom!" Clark shouted, running up to her, glancing back at the truck every third step. "Whose truck?"

Dropping the tools onto a tarp beside the tractor, Martha wiped her grimy hands on the front of her coveralls. "Yours," she replied casually, pulling a small note card from her pocket. "It's a gift from Lex Luthor." She handed the card to Clark.

"Dear Clark," he read, barely able to contain his excitement. "Always in your debt, the maniac in the Porsche." Looking up from the card, Clark gazed at the truck. "I don't believe it," he said, laughing. Then a serious question popped into his head, and he stopped laughing. "Where are the keys, Mom?"

"Your father has them," Martha explained, picking up her tools, turning back to the tractor engine.

Slipping the card into his pocket, Clark walked

quickly to the barn. He heard the deafening roar of the wood chipper before spotting his father operating the machine. Ear protection cut Jonathan off from everything but the dangerous task at hand. His thickly gloved hands shoved broken branches into the large opening on the top of the screaming machine, and a line of thinly shredded wood chips sprayed out the bottom.

Catching sight of Clark, Jonathan switched off the chipper and pulled off his ear coverings. Before Clark even opened his mouth, Jonathan answered all his questions and confirmed his worst fear.

"I know how much you want it, Clark," he began. "But you can't keep it."

"Why not?" Clark asked in disbelief, wondering if his father was going to deny him everything in life that might bring some fun or excitement, not to mention acceptance. "I saved the guy's life, Dad."

"So you think you deserve a prize?" Jonathan asked harshly, knowing Clark really didn't feel that way, but hoping it would derail some of his enthusiasm.

"That's not what I meant," Clark snapped back.

Jonathan turned back to his work, picked up another branch, and reached for the chipper's starter control.

Thinking quickly, Clark hit on a compromise plan he hoped might work. "Okay, what if you drive the new truck, and I drive the old one?" he proposed optimistically. "That way everybody wins."

"This isn't about winning, Clark," Jonathan replied, dropping the branch and walking away. From the day Clark had come into their lives, he and Martha had tried to teach the boy basic values, right from wrong, and what it took to be a man. At moments like this, his frustration in dealing with his unusual son overwhelmed any sense that Clark had actually turned out pretty well for a kid who dropped from the sky.

"Come on, Dad," Clark said, his own impatience growing with his father's stubbornness. "It's not like the Luthors can't afford it."

Jonathan stopped and turned around. "You want to know why that is?" he asked, walking back toward Clark. "Remember Mr. Bell? We used to go fishing on his land. And Mr. Guy, who used to give us pumpkins every Halloween? Lionel Luthor promised to cut them in on a deal that would give them control of their land while bringing them more money than they could ever hope to make farming. He sent them flashy gifts, too, but after they sold Luthor their farms, he went back on his word. Not only didn't he cut them in on the deal, but he evicted them, threw them right off the land their families had worked for generations."

"So you're judging Lex because of what his father did?" Clark asked, not buying Jonathan's argument.

"No, Clark," Jonathan replied, sighing. "I'm not judging Lex. I just want you to know where the money came from to buy that truck, that's all."

Realizing he was not going to win this argument, no matter how long it continued, Clark turned and stormed off toward the barn.

"Look, I know you're upset," Jonathan called after him. "It's normal."

Clark stopped, spun on his heels, then walked quickly toward his father. "Normal!" he shouted, his frustration reaching the boiling point. He was usually an even-tempered guy, the peacemaker during arguments, but the events of the past few days—not being allowed to join the football team, seeing Lana and Whitney on her porch, discovering his apparent power of invulnerability, and now this—had taken their toll. "Normal!" he repeated. "Is *this* normal?"

Moving swiftly, before Jonathan could fully comprehend his plan, Clark stepped up to the chipper, flipped on its powerful engine, and shoved his arm deep into the machine's churning mouth.

"Clark!" Jonathan shouted in horror, racing to the chipper as smoke and wood debris flew from the machine. Jonathan grabbed Clark's arm and wrenched it free from the razor-sharp, spinning blades. Staring down in amazement, Jonathan tried to comprehend the sight before him. Clark's shirt and jacket sleeves were shredded to ribbons, but his bare arm was completely unmarked, not a scratch to be seen. Jonathan looked at his son, confused and disoriented.

"I didn't dive in after Lex's car, Dad," Clark revealed. "It hit me at sixty miles an hour, knocked me through the guardrail, and sent me flying into the river. Now, does that sound normal to you?" Clark looked deep into his father's stunned eyes. "I would give anything to be normal. But I'm not."

Clark walked quickly into the barn and climbed the stairs to the hayloft, his retreat, his escape pod from the world. Glancing down at his telescope, he plopped down onto a hay bale and dropped his head into his hands.

Outside, Jonathan looked across the yard at Martha, who had stopped working on the tractor and had witnessed the latest demonstration of Clark's abilities, as well as the argument between father and son. She gestured with her head toward the barn, and Jonathan knew instantly that she was right. Returning a small nod of agreement, he headed in after Clark.

When Jonathan reached the hayloft, he found Clark with his knees clasped tightly to his chest. Neither said a word, then Jonathan dropped the mangled blade from the wood chipper on the floor right next to Clark. Its dull clanging startled the boy.

"I always knew this day would come," Jonathan said, kneeling next to his son and clasping his shoulder firmly. "Your mother and I both did. It's time, Clark."

"Time for what?" Clark asked silently, barely looking up.

"Time for the truth," Jonathan replied. "I want you to look at something." Jonathan pulled a small bundle wrapped in a soft cloth from his back pocket. Unwrapping the bundle, he handed Clark a rectangular metal plate, about the size of a paperback book. One side of the plate was covered in strange-looking symbols, which appeared to be writing of some kind but bore no resemblance to any written language ever seen on Earth.

"I think it's from your parents," Jonathan explained. "Your birth parents."

Taking the strange object from his father, Clark stared at the engraved symbols. "What does it say?" he asked.

"I have no idea," Jonathan replied. "I've been trying to decipher it for years. I've taken it to experts, but apparently it's not written in any language known to man."

Clark looked at his father skeptically. "What do you mean, not known to man?" he asked.

"Well, Clark, your real parents weren't exactly from around here," Jonathan pointed out

"Where are they from?" Clark asked, laughing nervously. His father glanced down at the telescope. "What are you trying to tell me, Dad, that I'm from another planet?"

Jonathan looked his son squarely in the eyes, but said nothing.

"Sure, Dad," Clark said, unable to hide the mixture of fear and annoyance in his voice. "And I suppose you stashed my spaceship in the attic, right?"

"Actually, it's in the storm cellar," Jonathan revealed, standing up. "Follow me."

Clark followed his father down the hayloft stairs,

across the barn, and out to a pair of angled metal doors leading to a low-ceilinged storm cellar. The cellar was a small space dug out of the earth, designed for a family to hunker down and wait out a tornado. When Clark was a kid, it had always made him think of *The Wizard of Oz,* Auntie Em and Uncle Henry hiding in the storm cellar when the twister hit, Dorothy unable to get down there in time.

He hadn't been down in their storm cellar in years. Still reeling from his father's announcement that the spaceship that brought him to Earth was stored down there, he wasn't too sure he wanted to venture down there right now.

Clark yanked on a pull chain, and the bare bulb in the ceiling blazed to life. Jonathan reached down to a dusty old tarp and whipped the large plastic sheet away, revealing a scarred metallic object resting on the dirt floor.

Kneeling down, Clark stared at the spaceship, a black oval about the size of a small kitchen table.

"This is how you came into our world," Jonathan revealed. "It was the day of the meteor shower. You fell right out of the sky, along with all those meteors, and crawled right into your mother's arms, as if it was destined to be."

Clark stood, then stepped back from the spaceship, his mind reeling. This couldn't be true. How could it be possible? He knew he had powers that others didn't have, but this?

"This is a joke, right?" was all he could think of to say.

"No, Clark," Jonathan replied. "It's not."

Anger replaced confusion in Clark's mind. "Why didn't you tell me this before?" he shouted.

"Because we wanted to protect you," Jonathan explained, realizing it sounded like a lame excuse as soon as he said it.

"Protect me from *what?*" Clark asked incredulously, turning away from his father. "You should have told me!" Before another word could be spoken, Clark sped up the stairs and raced from the farm as fast he could run, vanishing in a blur, fallen leaves swirling in mini-twisters behind him.

"Clark!" Jonathan yelled to the whirl of color and motion that was his son running at an unimaginable pace. *Useless,* he thought. *He's probably two counties*

*away from here by now. But what was I to do? I had
to tell him.*

Cornfields and farmhouses passed by on either side
of Clark in a melting collage of yellows and browns.
But no matter how fast he moved, he simply couldn't
run away from the startling truth about who he really
was.

CHAPTER 6

Lana Lang saddled up her beautiful brown-and-white horse, grabbed the bouquet of wildflowers she had picked earlier, and rode from her aunt's house, quickly entering a narrow path in the woods. Despite the fact that she made this journey every week, it never quite felt comfortable. Still, she could not imagine a week going by without paying her parents a visit.

After a short ride, the Smallville cemetery came into view. Thin wisps of fog drifted skyward toward a hazy moon glaring above the overgrown graveyard. Gnarled, twisted trees reached out with spiky, broken fingers, moss crept up the ancient headstones, and the wind howled eerily, sounding plaintive cries from those long gone.

Lana dismounted, clutching the flowers tightly, then shuffled through the tangled vines and crunching leaves toward the one place in the world where she felt a strong connection to the parents she barely knew.

The sharp snapping of a twig startled her. "Who's there?" she called out, looking around, spying a lone figure among the shadows.

"It's me," a trembling voice replied. "It's Clark."

"Clark Kent?" Lana asked, relieved, but very surprised to find her neighbor in this desolate place. "What are you doing creeping around the woods?"

"You'd never believe me if I told you," Clark answered in a weak, strained voice. "I didn't mean to scare you, Lana," he added, turning away.

"Clark, wait," Lana said, picking up something in his tone of voice that disturbed her. "I'm sorry. I didn't meant to accuse you of anything. I just wasn't expecting to see anyone out here."

Clark turned back toward Lana, and for the first time the moonlight caught his face, revealing red, puffy eyes and tears streaming down his cheeks.

"Are you okay?" she asked, unable to recall a time since they were little kids that she had seen Clark cry.

"Depends on what you mean by okay," Clark replied, choking back tears, his voice catching in his throat.

"Okay means better than average, not quite

excellent," Lana replied, smiling. "How's that for a definition?"

"I'm hanging out by myself in a graveyard," Clark pointed out. "Does that strike you as okay behavior?"

"Hey, I'm here, too, right?" Lana said.

"Good point," Clark agreed, sniffling and brushing away tears with his thumb. "So what's your story? What's a nice girl like you doing in a creeped-out place like this?"

Lana looked deep into Clark's red-rimmed eyes. Could she trust him? Of course. If there was anyone in her life she felt she could always trust, it was Clark—sure, steady Clark Kent. "Can you keep a secret?" she asked.

Clark smiled. *If you only knew,* he thought. *How would she take it if she knew that I was really a little green man from Mars or wherever? Would she freak out, run screaming, or just think I was nuts?*

"I'm the Fort Knox of secrets," he said softly.

"Okay then," Lana began, her eyes still locked onto his. "I came out here to talk with my parents. You must think I'm pretty weird, you know, conversing with dead people," she said, pointing to a well-groomed plot with a large, polished marble headstone.

Though still angry and confused about the day's startling revelation, Clark regained his composure. He loved talking with Lana, anytime, anywhere, even in a graveyard at night. "I don't think you're weird, Lana," he said, gently squeezing her shoulder and glancing down at the Langs' plot. "Do you remember them?" he asked.

"It's hard," Lana admitted. "They died when I was three. Sometimes I catch a glimpse in the back of my head, a quick image, a face, a piece of clothing, even a smell that seems familiar. I never would have thought it was possible to miss people I hardly knew."

"I'm sorry," Clark said, unable to think of anything insightful or comforting to say to ease Lana's pain.

"It's not your fault, Clark," Lana replied, looking over her shoulder at him. "Come on, I'll introduce you."

Cradling Clark's arm in her own, she led him the few steps to the Lang plot. By the hazy moonlight reflected on the gleaming stone, Clark could make out the carved words, which read: "LANG; LEWIS 1957–1989; LAURA 1959–1989."

Kneeling down close to the stone, Lana placed the

bouquet she had brought on the recently mowed grass at its base. Clark squatted, hands on his knees, a few feet behind her.

"Mom, Dad, this is Clark Kent," Lana said, smiling. Turning back to Clark she added, "Say hi."

"Hi," Clark said somewhat self-consciously, waving weakly at the headstone.

Turning back to the stone, Lana listened intently. "Yeah," she said after a few seconds. "He is kind of shy." She was silent for a few more moments. "How should I know?" she asked, continuing her conversation. Again, she looked over her shoulder at Clark. "Mom wants to know if you're upset about a girl," she said.

Clark shook his head and softly said, "No."

"Dad wants to know if something's wrong at school," Lana reported.

"No," Clark replied. "It's not that."

Lana's expression grew serious. "So, really, Clark, why are you out here?"

"Lana," he began, not quite sure what he would say, dying to tell her the truth but certain that he couldn't do that. "Do you ever feel like your life was supposed to be different from what it is?"

She nodded, looking at Clark wistfully. "Sometimes I dream that I'm at school, waiting for Nell, but she doesn't show up. But then my parents drive up instead, and they're not really dead, they're just really late. Then I get in their car and they take me back to my real life in Metropolis. That's when I usually wake up, and for a minute I'm totally happy. Until I realize that it was just a dream, and I'm still alone."

Lana's eyes welled up with tears. She hadn't expected to let so much out, so much honesty, so many secrets.

Seeing that she was upset, Clark stepped up next to her and kneeled beside her in front of the headstone. Jutting his chin out and tilting his head to one side, he listened. "What's that, Mrs. Lang?" Clark said after a moment.

He turned to Lana. "Your mom wants you to know that you're never alone. She also said that she's always watching over you, no matter what." Then he leaned in close to the stone. "What's that, Mr. Lang? Oh, yeah, and your dad thinks you're a shoo-in for Homecoming Queen."

Lana smiled broadly through her tears. "Did they really say that?" she asked.

"Sure," Clark replied, as they both stood up. "They're kind of chatty once you get them started."

Lana stood and squeezed Clark's hand. "I'm glad it was you creeping around in the cemetery. I've got to head home."

"Me, too," said Clark, walking beside her. "Mind walking? It's kind of an okay night."

"Sure," Lana replied, grabbing her horse's reins. Leading her horse, Lana set off back down the narrow path through the woods, with Clark beside her.

The walk home was quiet, with occasional small talk about school, Lana's aunt Nell, and the routine activities on the Kent farm. Before they knew it, Clark and Lana had emerged from the murky woods and were strolling down the road that separated their homes.

"Thanks for walking me home, Clark," Lana said when they reached the stone walkway leading to her house.

"It beats creeping around in the woods alone," Clark replied, shrugging.

"Do you realize that tonight we had the longest conversation we've ever had?" Lana asked, flashing an easy smile. "We should do it again."

"Yeah, we should," Clark replied, unable to think of

anything clever to say, thrilled that Lana wanted to get to know him. Emboldened by this compliment, Clark blurted out without thinking, "So, are you going to the dance?"

"Yeah," Lana answered quickly. "With Whitney."

Slick move, Kent! he thought instantly. *How dumb can you be!?* "Right, of course," he said aloud.

"How about you?" Lana asked. "You going?"

"Nah," Clark replied awkwardly. "I figured I'd sit it out." *Great! Let her know what a total loser you are, no date for the big dance.*

"Well, if you change your mind, I might save you a dance," Lana said. She leaned in close and kissed him gently on the cheek. "Good night, Clark."

Turning and strolling slowly toward home, Lana glanced over her shoulder, brightening Clark's night with her electric smile. Clark, wearing a broad grin of his own, filled with surprise and delight, headed across the dirt road to the Kent farm, practically floating above the ground.

Lana had kissed him. So what if it was only on the cheek? And she wanted to dance with him, and that smile. What started as the worst night of his life had ended up not so bad.

Or so Clark thought.

Peering from the shadows of Lana's front porch, Whitney had observed the touching exchange and genuine moment of friendship. His face tightened into an angry glare as he watched Clark's back recede into the darkness.

☞ ☞ ☞ ☞

Exhausted from the emotional roller-coaster of the day, Clark slept well that night. The following morning before school there was still the issue of returning the truck to Lex Luthor. As strongly as he resented his father's decision, Clark reluctantly went along with his wishes, agreeing to give back the truck, chalking up the disappointment to one more of life's little "hang in there" lessons.

Driving the truck slowly, to savor the few minutes it was actually his, Clark made his way to the edge of town, where he pulled up to the gates of the Luthor mansion and took in its surreal beauty.

Sprawled over many acres of prime Smallville real estate, the Luthors' gothic castle, its turrets silhouetted against a slate-gray sky, was unlike any other structure within hundreds of square miles. Looking completely out of place in rural America, its formal European gardens welcomed visitors, making them feel as if they had stepped back in time. The mansion itself, kept in pristine condition, appeared endless, its many peaked roofs capping impenetrable stone walls containing hundreds of identical windows.

Clark pressed a buzzer on the locked gate and received no reply. After looking around and making sure he was unseen, he grasped two thick metal bars in the middle of the gate and pulled them apart as if they were rubber bands, just wide enough to slip through. Once on the other side, he bent the bars back into their original positions and headed toward the house.

Clark would not have been shocked if a knight on horseback, a royal procession of kings and queens, or a captured damsel in need of rescuing had magically appeared as he made his way past tall trellises of climbing ivy and enormous stone pots filled with billowing flowers and fragrant herbs of every variety.

Upon reaching the massive studded wooden front door, he lifted the large obsidian door knocker and rapped several times. Dull thuds echoed through the thick doors. Receiving no answer—he half-expected a butler named Jeeves to open the door, a dour expression on his ancient face—Clark pushed open the doors and slipped inside.

The main hallway was dark, with walls covered with rich cherry wood and magnificent hand-carved stairways climbing in many directions. Completely confused as to where Lex might be, unsure if he was even home, Clark opted for the simplest greeting possible.

"Hello!" he yelled, the word echoing repeatedly off the polished wooden walls. Still no sign of life, as Clark walked straight down the hall toward a large set of double doors at its far end—what felt like miles from the front entrance.

As he approached, Clark heard a thin clanging of metal, repeated *chink-chink-chink* sounds, building in intensity, going silent, then resuming at an even faster pace. Slowly opening the doors, Clark slipped into the room.

In the massive parlor, two figures clad from head to toe in white, their faces covered by protective wire-mesh masks, were engaged in a fierce fencing match. Clashing swords were thrusting and blocking, with the occasional point finding its target. As the combatants danced around the room in a frenzied duel, Clark slipped behind an ancient suit of armor, partly embarrassed to have walked in on the match, and partly for protection from the battle, as the reality of his invulnerability was not yet an instinctive part of his thinking.

With a powerful flurry, one fencer pinned the other against a wall and thrust forward, touching the trapped fencer's midsection with the tip of the foil to claim victory. The loser angrily hurled his foil across the room, where it embedded into the wall beside the ancient armor, inches from Clark's head.

Pulling off his mask, the loser, now revealed to be Lex Luthor, stared at Clark in shock. "Clark," he said, concern and surprise in his voice. "I didn't see you."

"I buzzed, but nobody answered," Clark explained sheepishly.

"How did you get through the gate?" Lex asked, yanking his sword from the wall. He was a bit disturbed, but mostly puzzled by this breach in security.

"I kind of squeezed through the bars," Clark replied, then added quickly, "Is this a bad time?"

"Oh, no, no," Lex said as his opponent removed her

mask, causing flowing brown hair to cascade around her delicately featured face. "I think Haiki has sufficiently kicked my ass for the day." Lex tossed his sword, mask, and glove to Haiki, who gathered up the equipment and slipped silently from the room.

"This is a great place," Clark said politely.

"Yeah," Lex agreed sarcastically, "if you're dead and in the market for something to haunt."

"I just meant it's roomy, that's all," Clark said apologetically. Lex always made him feel like such a kid, even when he was being nice to him.

"It's the Luthor ancestral home," Lex explained. "My father had it shipped over from Scotland, stone by stone."

"I remember," Clark admitted. "The trucks rolled through town for weeks. Everyone was intrigued and excited, but then nobody moved in."

"My father had no intention of living here," Lex pointed out, grabbing a towel and wiping the sweat from his gleaming head and neck. "He's never even stepped through the front door."

"Then why did he ship it over?" Clark asked, following Lex toward the door.

"Because he could," Lex replied flatly. "The minute

he had it, he started looking for his next conquest. That's what my father does."

Lex strode quickly from the formal parlor to another room, which looked just as impressive to Clark—carved wood everywhere, a marble fireplace mantel—but was filled with exercise equipment, Lex's home gym set up in an arbitrary room among the fifty or more that filled the castle.

"How's the new ride?" Lex asked, tossing the towel aside and gulping down half a bottle of water, his back to Clark.

"That's why I'm here," Clark said, sad, but relieved to finally get to the point and dispense with the uncomfortable small talk.

"What's the matter?" Lex wondered. "You don't like it?"

"No, it's not that," Clark said quickly. "I can't keep it."

"Clark, you saved my life," Lex began. "I think it's the least I can do."

Clark looked down at the floor. There was simply nothing to say.

"Your father doesn't like me, does he?" Lex asked, turning to look right at Clark. "It's okay, I've been bald since I was nine. I'm used to people judging me before they get to know me."

"It's nothing personal," Clark said quickly. "He's just not crazy about your dad."

"I guess he figures the apple doesn't fall far from the tree," Lex said, pulling off his shirt and tossing it aside. "Understandable. How about you, Clark, did you fall far from the tree?"

"Most days I don't even feel like I'm from the same planet as my parents," Clark said, instantly regretting his little joke to himself.

"I know what you mean," Lex replied, nodding. "My father and I couldn't be more different. I only hope the people of this town will give me a chance to prove that."

Feeling very uncomfortable in this grand place, Clark turned to leave. "I better go," he said, handing the keys to Lex. "Thanks for the truck."

"Clark, do you believe a man can fly?" Lex asked suddenly.

"Sure," Clark answered, shrugging. "In a plane."

"No, I'm not talking about that," Lex said seriously. "I'm talking about soaring through the clouds, with nothing but air beneath you."

Clark sighed deeply. "People can't fly, Lex," he said impatiently.

"I did," Lex stated. "After the accident, when my heart stopped. It was the most exhilarating two minutes of my life. I flew over Smallville, and for the first time I didn't see a dead end. I saw a new beginning. And thanks to you, I've got a second chance." He looked Clark hard in the eyes. "We're the future, Clark, and I don't want anything to stand in the way of our friendship."

Clark nodded and left the room.

After stepping back out into the bleak morning, Clark passed through the gates—the conventional way this time—then headed down the road leading to the forest beside the Luthor mansion. He couldn't shake the feeling that Lex wanted something from him, but what? How could a guy who had everything need something from a guy who, well—lived on a farm and didn't even have his own truck?

Late for school as usual, Clark dashed through the woods, leaping over low twisted roots, dodging tree limbs at blinding speed, finally emerging from the dense forest, cutting into a nearby cornfield, and picking up his now familiar route to school.

ARRIVAL

As he ran, Clark wondered whether or not to tell Pete and Chloe about the truck, then decided he'd keep this, like so many other things in his life, to himself.

CHAPTER 7

When school let out that afternoon, Pete and Chloe headed downtown. Clark had some research to do in the school library and told the others he would catch up with them later.

Chloe was scheduled to cover the opening of a new discount store on Main Street started up by a local couple who hoped to draw shoppers back to the center of Smallville and away from a mall located forty-five minutes out of town. Not exactly what the Metropolis *Daily Planet* would consider big news, but the editor of the Smallville *Torch* realized it was a major event in the economic life of their town, and therefore worthy of coverage. Pete tagged along, jumping at any chance to spend time with Chloe, regardless of the reason.

Arriving on the scene, however, Chloe and Pete stepped into a much bigger story. A huge crowd had gathered in front of the Smallville Pharmacy. Sheriff's deputies rolled a comatose man out the front door on a stretcher, gently loading him into the back of a waiting ambulance.

"What happened here?" Chloe asked a man in the crowd, as she watched the stretcher disappear.

"Freddie Post, worked at the drug store," the man said in his slow rural drawl.

"Yeah," Chloe replied somewhat impatiently. "I know who he is. What happened?"

"In a coma," the local explained. "Electric shock, the sheriff said. No one's quite sure how it happened. Freddie was alone in the store."

Chloe turned to Pete. "He's the third victim this week," she reported. "The other two are up at the Smallville Medical Center, still in comas. They all suffered massive electric shocks. And here's the really weird part—they were all former high school jocks."

"Electric shock?" Pete repeated. "That's what happened to Assistant Principal Swan, too." Pete recalled how upset his family had been that a school official was attacked, and also that the school's trophy case, something of a Ross family shrine, had been defaced. "Turns out that Swan's okay, but he's got no memory of what happened. Do you know who the other two jocks were?"

"Tony Carozza and Wayne Higgins," Chloe said.

"Tony who works at Frank's Auto Repair, and Wayne who works at the post office?" Pete asked in amazement. "They were both on that great eighty-nine football team, along with Freddie Post."

"This has got to be more than a coincidence," Chloe said. "Especially here in Smallville, the weirdness capital of the world."

Pete's attention was drawn to an odd-looking man in the crowd. "Speaking of weird, who's that guy?" he asked, pointing at the tall man with the gaunt face and sunken eyes. "I've never seen him around here. I thought I knew everyone in town."

"I don't know," said Chloe, raising her digital camera. "Let's check him out." Chloe framed a close-up of the stranger, snapped the shot, then slipped the camera into her bag. "I think we should go back to the *Torch* office and do a little digging."

The two friends hiked back to the school, taking a well-trodden shortcut through the woods. When they reached the office of the *Torch*, Chloe unlocked the door, flipped on the lights, and turned on the paper's main computer.

"Pete, see if you can find a copy of the eighty-nine

yearbook," she said, while pulling the camera from her bag and directing Pete to a tall metal shelving unit on the opposite side of the room. "We may find some clues in there. Meanwhile, I'll download this shot onto the computer."

Within a few minutes, the image of the stranger in the crowd filled the computer's monitor, as Pete flipped through the dusty pages of the 1989 Smallville High yearbook.

"Chloe, look!" Pete shouted, pointing to a tiny black-and-white head shot among the sea of smiling faces making up the graduating class. "Look at this guy named Jeremy Creek."

Chloe looked closely at the photo in the yearbook, then back at the picture on the screen. "Whoa," she cried, pointing to the yearbook shot. "This is a picture of him twelve years ago." She turned to the color photo on the monitor. "And this is the one I just took a little while ago."

"He looks exactly the same," Pete observed. "He hasn't aged a day."

"Welcome to weird city!" Chloe exclaimed. "We have got to investigate this."

"I'm with you," Pete replied. "Let's get busy."

For the next few hours Pete and Chloe checked the Internet, dug through the *Torch*'s archives, and sent out a flurry of faxes. What they discovered seemed almost impossible, yet answered the many questions surrounding the mysterious attacks.

"Clark has got to see this," Pete said, finishing a newspaper clipping and shaking his head in disbelief.

"Why don't you go see if he's still in the library?" Chloe suggested.

"Be right back," Pete said, dashing out the door and down the hall.

Pete found Clark hard at work behind a stack of books in the library. Glad for the distraction and intrigued by Pete's freaked-out expression, Clark followed his buddy back to the newspaper office.

After recapping the events of the day for Clark, barely able to contain their excitement, Chloe and Pete finally showed him the two photos of Jeremy Creek.

"It's impossible," he said, gazing back and forth between the yearbook shot and the one on the computer monitor. "That can't be the same guy. He'd be like thirty today. It must be a kid who looks like him."

"My money was on the evil twin theory, too," Pete said, "until we got this back from the Missing Persons

Bureau." He handed Clark a fax. As Clark read, Chloe summarized the paper's contents.

"Jeremy disappeared from the State Infirmary a few days ago, where he'd been in a coma for twelve years," she explained. "He suffered from a massive electrolyte imbalance."

"That's why he hasn't aged a day," Pete continued.

"You're telling me he just woke up?" Clark asked skeptically. "Just like that?"

"No, there was a huge electrical storm," Chloe went on. "It knocked out the hospital's generator. When the power came back on, Jeremy was gone."

"The electricity from the storm must have charged him up like a Duracell," Pete concluded.

"And now he's back in Smallville putting former jocks into comas," Clark said, trying to make sense of all this. "Why?"

"Because twelve years ago today," Pete began, looking hard at Clark, "they chose Jeremy Creek as the Smallville High scarecrow."

"Check this out," Chloe said, handing Clark a yellowed newspaper clipping.

Clark read the headline aloud: "'Comatose boy found in field twenty yards from meteor strike.'"

"The exposure to the blast must have done something to his body," Chloe concluded, "enabling him to absorb and discharge electricity."

Clark shook his head and put down the clipping, the meaning of these events coming clear to him. *That boy was hanging in the field when the meteor landed . . . when I landed!* he thought. "No," he said abruptly. "This can't be right."

Pete turned to Chloe. "I think you better show him," he said, nodding toward a door across the office.

"Show me what?" Clark asked, still reeling from the terrible realization that somehow he might be responsible for all this.

"Follow me," Chloe said, crossing the office toward the newspaper's darkroom, followed closely by Pete, then Clark.

The three friends slowly opened the darkroom door and stepped inside. Light flooded the blackness. Chloe switched on a bare bulb, revealing a cluttered array of photographic enlargers, chemical trays, and a clothespin-laden line on which several prints hung drying. Chloe pointed at the wall on the far side of the room.

"It started out as a scrapbook and just kind of mutated," she said, walking toward the wall.

"What is it?" Clark asked, looking in amazement at a wall completely covered with newspaper clippings, magazine articles and covers, and photos.

"I call it the 'Wall of Weird,'" Chloe said proudly, gesturing with both hands at the floor-to-ceiling makeshift collage. "It's every strange, bizarre, and unexplained event that's happened in Smallville since the meteor shower. That's when it all began. That's when the town went schizo."

Stepping up to the wall, Clark scanned the collection in stunned disbelief, a growing, sickening sense of responsibility overwhelming his mind. Headlines in the *Smallville Ledger,* the local paper, screamed out "AREA MAN GAINS FINGER ON LEFT HAND—LOSES ONE ON RIGHT," "RIVER DREDGING UNCOVERS BIZARRE GLOW-IN-THE-DARK GEODES," and "TERMINALLY ILL WOMAN MIRACULOUSLY RECOVERS!" Stories of those directly affected by the explosive impact of the meteor strikes, and those who suffered from the bizarre aftereffects of the strange green-glowing rocks it deposited in Smallville, blanketed the entire wall.

All this because of the meteors landing, because of my landing here in Smallville, Clark thought in horror.

"So, what do you think?" Chloe asked, smiling, walking back toward Clark, unable to contain her pride and enthusiasm for the collection.

Clark's face turned pale. "Why didn't you tell me about this?" he said brusquely.

Stunned by the anger in his voice, Chloe turned her back on Clark and returned to the wall, her smile melting quickly into a scowl. "Do you tell me everything that goes on in your life?" she shot back defensively. "We all keep secrets, Clark."

Clark's eyes darted around the wall, taking in as much as they could, as quickly as his brain could process the information. Then one image leaped out at him. A *Time* magazine cover from the week following the meteor shower showed a close-up of a little girl dressed in a princess costume, her face streaked with tears, her eyes reflecting shock and sadness, a jeweled tiara on her head, a magic wand clutched tightly in her tiny fist. The headline read: "HEART-BREAK IN THE HEARTLAND."

Clark stared deeply into the child's eyes. What was it about that face?

Then it struck him like a thunderbolt, the realization bringing a wave of nausea and guilt flooding over his whole body. "Lana," he whispered, his heart aching for the little girl captured on film just seconds after witnessing the obliteration of her parents by flaming meteors.

"It's all my fault," Clark said, the words tumbling out without his even realizing it. The death of Lana's parents, the destruction of large sections of Smallville, and all the events captured so vividly on Chloe's Wall of Weird—all his fault.

He turned away and walked quickly from the dark-room, leaving Pete and Chloe staring at each other in puzzled silence.

Clark stormed down the hall, racing unsuccessfully to get away from the horrible images now burned into his brain. He ran right into the end of an evening pep rally for that weekend's football game.

Clark pushed through the crowd in the school's lobby, burst through the front doors, and bounded down the stone stairs. He walked briskly, with no idea where he was headed.

A hand from behind grabbed him on the shoulder. "Chloe, leave me alone," Clark said before he had turned around. "I'm having a really bad day!"

The powerful hand spun Clark around, and he found

himself face to face with Whitney. "Well, it's about to get worse," Whitney said, tightening his grip. "Congratulations, Clark. You're this year's scarecrow."

Enraged, Clark slammed Whitney's hand away. "Don't mess with me right now!" he snarled, thinking how much he would love to pound the jock's face into mush.

"Come on, bring it on," Whitney challenged him, enjoying the idea of a one-on-one battle with the man vying for Lana's affections. Whitney yanked off his jacket and spread his arms wide, gesturing for Clark to make the first move.

The years of keeping his powers hidden from the world, the lectures from his father about resisting the temptations of showing off what he could do, and the restraint that he had proudly shown, believing it was best, all vanished in a moment of pure fury.

Clark drew back his fist and stepped forward, launching a punch right at Whitney's chest. Before the punch landed, Clark felt all the energy in his body drain, as he lost his balance and fell weakly toward the ground, clutching at Whitney's shirt for support.

Tearing the shirt open as he fell, Clark spied Lana's

necklace around Whitney's neck, its shimmering green stone dangling from the silver chain.

"What's going on with you and Lana?" Whitney demanded. He wrenched Clark's hand from his shirt and shoved him to the ground.

"Nothing's going on," Clark replied, crumbling to the blacktop in a heap, sweat covering his pale forehead and temples.

Glowering over Clark, Whitney noticed him staring at the bright-green stone.

"You like Lana's necklace, huh?" Whitney taunted Clark. He leaned down close, unfastened the necklace from his own neck, and placed it around Clark's. "Well, enjoy it, because that's as close as you're ever going to get to her!"

The tiny green stone rested on Clark's throat. Growing weaker by the second, all thoughts of fighting back or even of struggling to his feet vanished, replaced by the single worry of how to remain alive.

Wave upon wave of darkness quickly overcame him, and within minutes Clark blacked out.

The crowd from the pep rally had dispersed. A pickup truck screeched to a halt a few feet from where Clark lay sprawled on the empty parking lot blacktop.

Two of Whitney's teammates, proudly clad in their Smallville High letterman jackets, leaped from the truck's cab. The three jocks gathered up Clark's motionless body and dumped it into the truck's bed, then squeezed in next to the driver, who peeled out, swiftly vanishing from sight.

Hidden behind the thick trunk of a nearby maple tree, having silently witnessed the entire abduction, Jeremy Creek stood, his sad eyes capturing every detail as his tortured soul relived the events that had taken place on this day, twelve years earlier.

CHAPTER 8

Clark regained consciousness slowly. The sound of wind rustling through cornstalks penetrated the fog inside his head first, followed by the sensation of chills running across his chest, arms, and legs. When he finally forced his leaden eyelids open, Clark was confused by the sight before him.

High off the ground, he peered over the tops of tall stalks in a cornfield. He was unable to keep his head up, and his chin dropped to his chest, which was bare and covered with a large red letter "S," painted in sloppy, slashing, violent brushstrokes. Naked except for his boxer shorts, Clark sweated, shivered, and struggled for breath in the misty, chilly night air of late October, his pale body illuminated by cool blue moonlight.

Trying to move his arms, Clark felt them restrained, bound by thick ropes under each armpit. The ropes were tied around a wooden stake, from which he dangled, limp and drained.

Why can't I break free? he thought through the thick haze of exhaustion and the pounding pain in his head. Struggling against the ropes again, he failed to budge them. He should have been able to snap the ropes as if they were thin blades of grass. After all, he could snap thick metal pipes like twigs. So why, why was he so weak, so very tired?

Then Clark remembered the necklace.

Painfully twisting his neck, sweat dripping from the swath of black hair matted on his forehead, he caught a glimpse of the green jewel bobbing near his throat, and the events leading up to this moment came rushing back with ferocious clarity.

Images flashed through his mind in rapid succession—his confrontation with Whitney, his weak, ineffective punch, the shackling around his neck of this tiny green stone, and finally, the announcement that he had been selected to be this year's scarecrow, to endure the annual humiliation of the weak and unpopular, or in his case of a perceived threat to Whitney's exclusive relationship with Lana.

He thought of all the times he came close to Lana, only to break out in a sweat, grow dizzy, or simply collapse. When he went to punch Whitney, his blow fell weakly away, and now he hung here helplessly, when he should have easily broken free of the ropes. Something about this small green stone made him sick. He vowed to figure this all out . . . if he ever got down from here alive.

With great difficulty Clark lifted his head to search for some way out of this, just as a tall, thin figure silhouetted by the moonlight stepped from the stalks and stopped at Clark's feet.

"It never changes," the ghostly figure said, looking up, his face showing no reaction to the sight of a half-naked young man hanging in the dark.

"P-please help me," Clark stammered, unsure whether or not he was imagining this encounter.

"It hurts, doesn't it?" the figure commented, ignoring Clark's plea. "They don't care, but it does hurt."

Fighting to keep his eyes open, Clark stared down at the stranger. The image of a black-and-white yearbook photo flashed into Clark's mind, and he suddenly recognized the eerie figure before him.

"You-you're Jeremy," Clark gasped, his voice trembling, sweat dripping from his lower lip.

"I haven't been Jeremy since the day they hung me up there," the troubled young man began, his voice even and emotionless. "Jeremy was a quiet kid waiting for high school to end, so the rest of his life could begin. But that never happened."

Jeremy paused and glanced around the cornfield. Memories of that terrible day flooded his mind, but his face revealed nothing of the turmoil within.

"I thought if I punished them, it would stop," he explained, as much to himself as to Clark. "But it never stops." He turned and stepped away.

"Wait," Clark called out weakly, his warm, foggy breath billowing in the cool air. "Where are you going?"

Jeremy stopped. "To the homecoming dance," he replied, smiling sardonically. "I never made it to mine."

"Get me down, please," Clark groaned, struggling to stay conscious, the pain in his shoulders almost unbearable.

Jeremy shook his head. "You'll be safer here," he said, vanishing into the cornfield.

As Clark dangled helplessly in a half-dream state, Jeremy Creek walked quickly through the field, soon emerging onto the road that led to Smallville High and just happened to border the LuthorCorp fertilizer plant.

୭ ୭ ୭ ୭

Lex Luthor sped from the plant's parking lot and tore onto the road, his headlights illuminating the cornfield that ran alongside. After only seconds on the road, Lex caught sight of someone in his lights, crouching at the edge of the rows of corn. He slammed on his brakes and skidded to a stop, then stared at the thin, nervous-looking figure.

What was so familiar about this kid? *I know this guy,* Lex thought. *But how? From where?*

The memory struck Lex like an electric jolt searing through his brain, shaking his body. In that earth-shattering moment, twelve years earlier, in this very cornfield, Lex saw this young man, who now somehow stood in his headlights, hanging from a post in the field. The image of the red "S" painted on his chest, the desperation etched in the boy's face, and Lex's own terror all flooded back to him now.

More images came—the trail of black smoke in the sky, the tremendous explosion, a blinding flash of light, and then the cloud, that horrible wall of thick gray smoke that swept across the cornfield, destroying everything in its path. First, the boy on the post slammed face-first into the ground, then Lex himself, overwhelmed, engulfed, absorbed by the devastation, his life forever changed.

Snapping back to the present, Lex grabbed a flashlight and scrambled from his car. His mind was racing, as he tried to figure out what that kid was doing here, and how he could possibly look the same as he had back then.

The flashlight beam played on the cornstalks, but the boy was gone. Lex stood alone on the dark road, then switched off his light and turned back to the car. That's when he heard a faint cry from the interior of the cornfield.

"Help me," the strained voice cried, drifting on the wind. "Help me, please."

This is too weird! Lex thought, echoes of the scene twelve years earlier reverberating in his head. But this was real, this was now. Someone was in trouble.

Lex flipped his flashlight back on and pounded into the cornfield, sweeping the beam left and right, until he saw it—a boy tied to a post, red "S" shining from his glistening chest. Stepping closer, shining the beam on the boy's face, Lex realized who it was.

"Clark!" he shouted, hurrying behind the post. "Oh, my God!"

Lex quickly untied each rope. "Who did this to you?" he asked, his stiff fingers fumbling in the cold.

"It doesn't matter," Clark groaned, feeling his arms finally released from their torturous bonds.

As Lex eased Clark down from the post, Lana's necklace caught on a splintered section, snapped open, and tumbled to the ground. Clark landed on his feet, strength and alertness already returning. He dashed to his clothes, which were piled nearby, left in a heap by the jocks who had strung him up.

"Clark, you need to see a doctor," Lex said, genuine concern in his voice.

In the time it took for Clark to gather up his clothes, he had regained all his strength and mental focus. This happened each time he removed himself from close proximity to the necklace, but he still never got used to the swiftness with which his strength returned.

"I'll be okay. Thanks, Lex," he said, clutching his bundle of clothes and dashing into the corn rows, bursting with energy and hoping he was not too late.

"At least let me give you a ride!" Lex called after

him, but he got no response. The night was again silent, and Clark had vanished.

As he was turning to leave, Lex's light found the fallen necklace. Squatting, he picked it up, curiously examining it in the flashlight beam, which refracted through the dense gem and sent sharp fingers of green light spreading in all directions.

Lex stood up and shrugged. Then he slipped the necklace into a pocket and headed back to his car.

☞ ☞ ☞ ☞

At the homecoming dance in the gym at Smallville High, couples swayed back and forth as the sound of "Maybe," by the Stereophonics, filled the carefully decorated room, transforming the gym into an enchanted ballroom. For one evening the students gathered there were not guys and girls, jocks and nerds, cheerleaders and brainiacs, but rather regal ladies and gentlemen of the court.

Lana Lang and Whitney Ellsworth, Smallville's newly crowned Homecoming Queen and King, danced slowly, their bodies close, hands clasped. They stared lovingly into each other's eyes, searching for their futures, heads adorned with their official crowns, Whitney's tux covered by his kingly sash, Lana's gown flowing like water as she glided across the dance floor.

Outside, Chloe sat on the school's front steps, listening to the music and chatter drifting through the half-opened door. Clark had never actually asked her to the dance, but she couldn't believe he wouldn't even show up.

"Why don't you come inside?" said a gentle, familiar voice behind her.

Pete, who was always there. Pete, whom she took for granted. Unlike Clark, he had actually asked her to the dance, as a "friend-friend thing" she recalled. Sweet Pete, too shy to ask her for a real date and happy just to be around her.

"You know that Clark's not going to show," Pete said, almost reading her thoughts.

Chloe sighed deeply, then stood up and smiled, realizing that Pete was right. "Wanna dance?" she asked.

Pete's heart soared, but, as usual, he expressed himself through humor. "After you, m'lady," he said, bowing deeply, one arm across his waist, the other gesturing toward the door.

Neither friend was really that comfortable on the dance floor, especially when it came to a slow dance, but neither cared as they held each other and moved with the crowd. Pete extended his arm, spinning Chloe like a ballerina, then pulled her back, both of them giggling.

As the happy couples danced the night away, just outside a lone figure crept through the darkness, a crowbar dangling from his clenched fist. Jeremy Creek made his way to the back of the school. He stopped before a large red metal box mounted on the wall. The box was labeled "FIRE SPRINKLER SYSTEM—EMERGENCY ACCESS ONLY."

Jeremy pried open the doors to the sprinkler system with a crowbar and peered into the mass of wiring, hoping to find a way to activate the system.

"Jeremy," called a voice, startling the intent young man. "You need to stop this." Jeremy stepped around the open door, and squinted at the figure silhouetted by a parking lot lamppost. *Who is this, foolish enough to confront me? Haven't I shown them enough of my power? Haven't I shown them what I am capable of?*

As the figure stepped toward him, Jeremy recognized the boy as the poor soul he had just seen hanging in the cornfield, this year's scarecrow, now fully clothed and apparently no worse for his ordeal.

"I don't know how you got here," Jeremy said, tossing aside the crowbar and sending it clanging to the blacktop. "But you should have stayed away."

"I won't let you hurt my friends," Clark Kent stated firmly, approaching Jeremy.

"Those people in there aren't your friends," Jeremy cried. "I have a plan. The sprinklers will get them nice and wet, then I'll handle the rest."

"They never did anything to you," Clark pointed out, stopping right in front of the agitated young man.

"I'm not doing this for me!" Jeremy cried out in surprise. "I'm doing this for *you,* and for all the others like us!"

What happened to you was my fault, Clark thought, taking the full brunt of responsibility for all the strange and terrible things caused by the meteor shower. "I can understand your pain," he said.

Jeremy laughed. "I'm not in pain," he said, turning away from Clark. "I have a gift and a purpose, and a destiny."

When Jeremy completed his turn, he was shocked

to find Clark, suddenly, impossibly in front of him again, blocking his path.

"So do I," Clark explained. "And I'm not going to let you hurt anyone else."

Moving swiftly, Jeremy grabbed Clark's shoulders, sending searing jolts of electric current surging into his body. Clark reached out, snatched Jeremy by the arms, and flung him away, sending him crashing onto the hood of a nearby pickup truck.

"Give it up, Jeremy," Clark demanded.

Jeremy scrambled to his feet and slammed his palm down fiercely onto the truck's hood, sending a charge through the metal. The engine roared to life.

Jeremy slipped behind the wheel and floored the truck. Its squealing tires left rubber as its massive body sped right at Clark, who set his legs apart and extended his arms to stop the onrushing vehicle.

KA-RUNCH!

Clark caught the truck's grill, his fists crushing its thick metal spikes. Tensing his muscles, pressing his heels into the ground, Clark slowed the truck, as Jeremy, peering through the windshield, shocked by the astounding display of power before him, let up on the gas.

Confused and angry, Jeremy mashed the accelerator to the floor and caught Clark—who had relaxed his muscles for a moment—off guard. The truck screeched into motion again, Clark firmly clamped onto its grill.

Unable to regain his footing, Clark was helplessly pushed backward toward a brick wall, like a giant hood ornament on a truck destined for destruction. Protruding from the ground just in front of the brick wall, a water-main pipe stood five feet tall, painted bright red.

CRASH!!!

Enraged beyond reason, Jeremy rammed the truck into the wall, snapping off the water-main pipe and tearing a hole in the floor of the truck's cab, just before he slammed through the bricks using Clark's body as a battering ram.

The truck finally came to rest, half inside, half out, having opened a huge hole in the wall, with Clark still attached to the grill. Water shot from the broken pipe, flooding into the cab and pouring across the floor of the building.

Spotting the rising pool of water near his feet, Jeremy desperately tried to open his door, which was pinned shut by the edge of the hole he had created upon impact. When the water finally reached his feet, electricity surged from Jeremy's body and, conducted by the water, flowed into the metal body of the truck.

THOOM!!

Clark exploded from the truck and was catapulted into the air by a powerful jolt of electrical energy that slammed him into the far wall. He watched in horror as the electricity in Jeremy's body drained into the vehicle, while Jeremy slumped over the steering wheel.

Clark raced to the truck, grabbed the front fender, and pulled, rolling the vehicle forward just enough to free the door. Clark reached the driver's door and tore it from its hinges, just as the last volt left Jeremy's body, sizzled in a crackling blue arc, and vanished into the dashboard.

Jeremy stared up at Clark, his face calm but haggard.

"You okay?" Clark asked, slightly out of breath.

Jeremy nodded. "Who are you?" he asked in a soft voice, sounding like the boy he had been twelve years earlier. "And where am I?"

As Clark stared at him he realized that the memory of the last few minutes, and quite possibly longer than that, had been wiped clean. "I'm Clark Kent, and you're in Smallville."

Jeremy looked at Clark, confused, yearning for answers but too exhausted to pursue them now. "I want to go home," was all he said.

Clark nodded and helped him from the truck.

☙ ☙ ☙ ☙

As the homecoming dance wound down, Clark watched from the shadows of the gym's upper level. The crowd on the dance floor had dwindled to just a few. Pete and Chloe had long since left, but the king and queen still held court in the center of the floor, Lana's jeweled tiara sparkling in the dim light of the gym, as it did all those years ago above the tear-stained face of the little girl on the cover of *Time*. A spotlight caught the couple just as they shared a passionate kiss intended to last a lifetime.

Clark stared down at them. Why did he do this to himself? Now more than ever he knew he could never be with Lana, not after what he did to her parents. Still, his heart ached at the thought of not having her in his life.

Confused and tired, he turned and left the gym. Out in the parking lot, Clark spied three identical pickup trucks parked alongside one another. *Whitney and his buddies,* Clark thought. *They probably all played with matching toy trucks when they were little.* Then a mischievous grin spread across his face as an idea suddenly popped into his head.

Glancing around to make sure he was alone, Clark moved swiftly. He lifted one truck over his head and slid the massive pickup onto the second, then hoisted the third onto the top of the stack. Chuckling to himself as he slipped into the bushes to admire his handiwork from a distance, Clark got a kick out of the perfect pile of identical vehicles, though he could only imagine what his father would say at this blatantly risky display of his power.

Kids drifted out of the school in twos and threes, each group stopping to stare at the stack of trucks, pointing and laughing. Whitney emerged from the building, his arm around Lana. Catching sight of his truck buckling under the weight of the other two trucks perched above it, Whitney's jaw fell open, and his arm dropped to his side.

"Who did this to my truck!" he screamed red-faced

and furious, above the laughter of a group of students nearby.

Lana couldn't help but smile at this bizarre, silly sight. She glanced away for a moment and caught a quick glimpse of what looked like Clark disappearing into a cornfield.

Jeweled points of light twinkled in the inky blackness, brought closer by the lens of Clark's telescope. In the barn's hayloft, Clark perused the night sky, thinking of his true home, wondering if he would ever learn more about the world from which he had come.

Startled by the sound of footsteps scraping up the wooden ladder leading to the loft, Clark lifted his face from the lens and saw his father's head poke above the loft's floorboards.

"I remember when you asked me for that," Jonathan said, pointing at the telescope and taking a seat next to Clark. "You were ten. I should have told you the truth then."

Clark looked at his father but remained silent.

Jonathan continued: "Your grandfather gave me that telescope when I was about your age. I came down to breakfast one morning and there it was. I could tell something was wrong with Dad. That's when he told me he'd been fighting cancer for a year. Two weeks later he was dead."

Jonathan looked deep into Clark's eyes. "I swore I'd never keep secrets from my own son," he said. "But now I have, and I'm sorry."

"He was just trying to protect you," Clark replied, glad that his father had come to him.

"I know," Jonathan said. "But I was still angry with him, and I understand if you're still angry with me."

An uncomfortable silence passed between them.

"No more secrets, Clark," his father finally said. "I promise."

Clark nodded, indicating that he accepted his father's apology, knowing this was not easy for Jonathan, whose pride and stubbornness sometimes got in his way.

"You okay?" Jonathan asked.

"Can I answer that in about five years?" Clark replied, smiling.

"Oh, I almost forgot," Jonathan said, pulling a small metal box from his jacket pocket. "Lex stopped by a little while ago. He left this for you with a note. I guess he still feels he owes you something for saving his life. At least this gift fits in your pocket." Handing the box and an envelope to Clark, he stood and stepped back onto the ladder.

"See you in the morning," Jonathan said, starting down.

"Dad," Clark stopped him, placing the box and note on the floor. "I'm glad you and Mom are the ones that found me."

"We didn't find you, Clark," Jonathan said, Martha's voice echoing from long ago. "You found us." Then he shimmied down the ladder and walked from the barn.

Clark looked at the metal box his father had handed him. Raised straps ran the length of the box, with chrome studs protruding every few inches. In the center of the lid, a silver medallion shone, carved with characters Clark didn't recognize.

Opening the envelope, he read the note:

Clark, you dropped this. Thought I'd return it with an additional little gift. Please keep the box as a token of our growing friendship. My mother gave it to me when I was little. She bought it in the Casbah in Morocco. The guy who sold it to her said it was made from a soldier's armor. It's made of lead. In any case, it's yours. I hope you're okay. The note was signed, *Best wishes, L.L.*

Clark put the note aside and slowly opened the box. Instantly, he felt weak as the green glow from Lana's necklace washed over him. After snapping the lid shut and placing the box on the floor, he felt better at once. Somehow this lead box protected him from the harmful effects of the stone. Lead. He would have to remember that.

Lana's necklace, he thought. *Lex must have found it in the field. I should return it to her, but I can't let her see how it affects me.* Then the image of Lana's face blocked all other thoughts from his mind. Clark flipped on the boom box he kept in the hayloft, and music echoed throughout the barn. He peered back into the telescope.

"I didn't see you tonight, Clark," said a soft voice, startling him.

Looking up, Clark saw Lana, radiant in her gown, standing right there in the hayloft. "Lana?" he said, stunned by her unexplained but entirely welcomed appearance. "What are you doing here?"

She walked slowly toward him, placed one hand on his hip, and clasped his hand with the other. "I saved that dance for you," she explained.

Clark accepted her into his arms timidly, and they

swayed in time to the music. Their eyes met as they moved, and Lana gazed up at him, smiling.

"Is everything okay, Clark?" she asked sweetly.

He smiled back, feeling completely happy. "Perfect," he replied, closing his eyes, savoring the moment . . .

. . . A magical moment that was abruptly shattered by the blaring of car horns. Clark's eyes popped open, revealing that he was alone. *She wasn't really here. Just in my mind. Oh, Lana. LANA!*

A second round of horn honking snapped him back to reality. Looking down from the hayloft, he spotted three cars filled with reveling homecoming partygoers. In the back seat of the last car sat Lana, obviously about to be dropped off at home.

The necklace. Clark grabbed the box. Moving impossibly fast, he raced down the ladder, across the road, and up onto Lana's porch, where he swiftly pulled the necklace from the box and hung it on the screen door's knob with such speed that he barely felt the effects of the stone. Clark slipped the box into his pocket and flashed back across the road and up to the hayloft, just as Lana climbed from the car.

The entire journey took less than three seconds, but Clark was not the least bit out of breath. He watched as Lana waved good-bye to her friends, who drove away, still honking. Then she turned and stepped up onto the porch.

Reaching the front door, Lana's eyes lit up, spotting the necklace. She lifted it gently from the doorknob and fastened the clasp around her neck, thinking how terribly romantic it was for Whitney to have arranged for it to be waiting for her after their magical evening together. She opened the door and stepped inside, never more in love with her wonderful boyfriend.

"Good night, Lana," Clark said softly as her screen door slammed shut. "Thanks for the dance."

SMALLVILLE™

SPEED

By Cherie Bennett
and Jeff Gottesfeld

Smallville is suffering a spate of apparently unmotivated racial attacks. But despite obvious injuries, none of the victims seem able to recall how the assaults happened. It's as though the perpetrator is invisible. As Clark Kent investigates for the school paper, he discovers a student with a definite racial chip on his shoulder, and the kind of unnatural abilities that are perfectly suited to a campaign of terror. Carl has acquired the power of supernatural speed and is using it to attack his victims between moments in time. Now his sights are set on burning down Smallville's interracial church, and Clark is the only one who can stop him . . .

www.atombooks.co.uk

SMALLVILLE™

SECRETS
By Suzan Colon

Clark Kent has a serious crush, and for once it's not Lana Lang who's the focus of his dreams. He's fallen for Lilia Sanchez, his Spanish teacher. Lilia is unlike anyone Clark has ever met. In fact, Clark suspects she might be telepathic. She certainly seems to know a lot of his classmates' secrets. And, following a freak accident, discovers some pretty revealing stuff about Clark too. Suddenly Clark's extraordinary double life is in danger of being blown, and to make matters worse, Lilia is spending a lot of time in the company of the last person who should learn the truth: Lex Luther.

www.atombooks.co.uk

SMALLVILLE™

SEE NO EVIL

By Cherie Bennet
and Jeff Gottesfeld

Clark Kent has somehow got himself cast as
lead man in the new school play. It was
hardly intentional, but he's too good a guy to
blow everyone out. Besides, he gets to play
opposite a girl who'd be his choice for leading
lady any time—the gorgeous Lana Lang. But
pretty soon Clark's worried about more than
just stage fright. Someone in school has taken
a serious dislike to the production, beginning
a murderous rampage designed to bring the
curtain down . . . permanently.

www.atombooks.co.uk

SMALLVILLE™

STRANGE VISITORS

By Roger Stern

Spiritual guru Donald Jacobi announces that fragments from Smallville's famed glowing meteorites are the key to eternal health and cosmic strength. Setting up a website to sell the green rocks, Jacobi soon amasses a fortune . . . and a startling control over his desperate followers. Investigating these events, Clark discovers that fraud and dashed hopes are the least of the dangers the rocks pose. But can he find a way to stop Jacobi—before the transforming power of the meteors is spread around the world?

www.orbitbooks.co.uk

SMALLVILLE ™

DRAGON
By Alan Grant

Clark Kent's powers have completely vanished. Worse still, he has no memory of them. As if on cue, a recently paroled murderer rolls into town. Ray Dansk is a man burning with rage—and it's focussed on the people who sent him down. Unless Clark's memory and abilities return, Smallville will be at the mercy of a psychopath who's feeling more than a little physically-enhanced thanks to a drop of meteor-contaminated water . . .

www.orbitbooks.co.uk

SMALLVILLE™

HAUNTINGS
By Nancy Holder

Ginger's family know all about the rumours of ghosts when they take on the farmhouse near Clark and Lana's homes. What they don't realise is that weird stuff in Smallville usually equates with Seriously Dangerous. Something has transformed these particular phantoms into sinister engines of vengeance, and pretty soon Clark, Lana and Ginger are all that stand in their path. But will Clark's developing superpowers be of any use in a battle against disembodied spirits of the dead . . . ?

www.orbitbooks.co.uk

SMALLVILLE ™

WHODUNNIT
By Dean Wesley Smith

While searching for a missing friend, Clark, Lana, and Chloe make a horrible discovery—an entire family, gruesomely murdered. At the same time, Lex Luthor's tycoon father is violently abducted in broad daylight. Two desperate quests to solve these crimes begin, but neither Clark's superpowers nor Lex's great wealth can help. Innocent lives will depend on Clark's and Lex's relentless determination to unravel the mysteries before a savage murderer strikes again—and Lionel Luthor is killed by his sadistic captors.

www.orbitbooks.co.uk